CLOSE FOLLOW

July 15, 2022

Alex A

Thank you for your interest in my book!

I just finished the Rough draft of book II!

Enjoy this fast paced trip!

Doug Emery

CLOSE FOLLOW

Doug Emery

Waterside Productions

Cover Design by: OnTheBrinkCreative.com

PUBLISHER'S NOTE:
This book is a work of fiction. Names, characters, places, and incidents either are the product of the author's imagination or used fictitiously, and any resemblance to actual persons, living or dead, events, or locales is entirely coincidental.

Printed in the United States of America

First Printing, 2021

ISBN-13: 978-1-956503-41-8 print edition
ISBN-13: 978-1-956503-42-5 ebook edition

Waterside Productions
2055 Oxford Ave
Cardiff, CA 92007
www.waterside.com

DEDICATION

I dedicate this book to Joey Madia. Without you as my editor, mentor, and guide, there would be nothing but tablets of thoughts and ideas scattered about. You made this wildly fun!

"I only have one rule: No felonies!"

~ Trevor McCowen

TABLE OF CONTENTS

ACKNOWLEDGMENTS

I want to thank:

My wife, Melissa, for patiently waiting to continue a conversation, dinner, or car ride, and for forgiving the midnight note-taking sessions when the ideas spurred me to get thoughts on paper. Plus, for her own creative genius and day job for never-ending fodder.

My daughters, for their excitement and enthusiasm for family range days.

My staff, for all of the "Line 6" (duties as otherwise assigned) that come up, including proofreading; juggling the many tasks of my diverse, full life; and keeping my work life in good order.

The law enforcement officers who train through my organization—North Coast Peace Officer Training Foundation—for their personal dedication to serve and protect their communities and come home safe each night.

The men I work armed security jobs with and train beside, for your stories and the shared experiences we have had.

The pre-publication readers who provided technical expertise and shared personal experiences for accuracy and authenticity.

Each of you is a part of this story.

PROLOGUE
THIS ISN'T LIKE IN THE MOVIES

Let's start with an introduction. My name is Trevor McCowen. In many ways I'm a regular guy, though, as you'll see, my life is often not. I like to mix things up—personal and business, philosophy and firearms.

We are just finishing a day of employee firearms training. Security officers and law enforcement personnel were all sitting around unwinding after a day on the range.

To me, these moments can be the best of the experience—someone will start a story, or a couple guys who have worked together in the past will joke about a strange occurrence they shared. This sort of relaxed sharing provides a real glimpse into each of these men's lives, which helps me to train them. After all, that's why they're here.

Sure enough, within minutes, someone starts a story. Bill—whose call sign is Soup, because of his last name—is a great storyteller. It's like a movie unfolding in front of you—rich and full of detail.

"This is the late 1970s. We are standing on a little local airstrip over in the next county. I can hear the plane's single engine prop well before I can see it. It's off to the east and the sun is hanging low in the western sky. 'Here it comes boys!' I say. 'Time to look sharp.' The five of us all turn toward the sound of the engine.

"I am new to the county sheriff's office, and not at all sure how I got drawn for this assignment. As to the other four guys, one is from my county task force, although we had never met prior to this assignment. Two are task force guys from the county we are standing in, and the last is a township officer, also from our county, whose department took the informant call from the pilot.

"We are all in plain clothes, handguns only, and protective vests. Plain clothes means different things to different officers. But it was the '70s, so sport coats for all but the township guy—he had on a dark blue wind breaker.

"This pilot gets a call from some local Youngstown men who are asking for a private flight home from the east coast. Because it's a small plane the pilot asks a lot of questions about how heavy these men are and what luggage they are bringing with them. They say they will need to call him back with the weight and size of the luggage.

"One of the men rings back thirty minutes later with the weight of their luggage—three duffle bags, weight eleven, seventeen, and fourteen pounds, dimensions sixteen by twenty-six inches, roughly all the same size, and a larger item—forty-eight by twenty-four by sixteen inches, weight fifty-five pounds. The pilot says, 'That's a big suitcase.' The guy replies with 'Think of a bale of hay.' And that is *exactly* what the pilot thought, so he called the township department, who in turn called us. Because this runway is in the next county over, we needed to call that sheriff's office for permission and they wanted to send out support as well and take credit for the arrest.

"Anyhow ... The sun is low in the horizon, with no wind. The plane comes in smoothly and taxies up to the hangers we are standing in front of. The pilot shuts down the engine and opens his door. Then the back door comes open and the two guys start to get out.

"The five of us converge on the little plane, guns in one hand, badges in the other, looking more like Feds than local SO and township PD.

"The plane holds the three duffle bags with their clothing—and fifty thousand dollars, all in twenties. It surprised me how little room that much money took up ... just five stacks not much more then three inches tall and only weighing like five pounds.

"The big ticket was the bale of hay ... Well, actually, it was a real bale of *marijuana*! I had never in my life even seen a *photo* of a bale of pot! It was stuffed in a couple of garbage bags and taped up tight.

"We cuff up everyone, including the pilot—we want to protect him as the informant—and haul them all down to the county we are standing in for processing.

"The pilot gets cut loose and the other two are booked for possession with intent to distribute.

"We do all the paperwork and go home feeling really good about the day's work. A few days later, however, I get called into the SO's office, where I'm informed that the two guys hired Silverberg as their defense attorney. Attorney Silverberg called the judge who is handling the case and requested the fifty thousand be returned to Silverberg for his clients, because it was not part of the drug operation. The cash was in the men's personal clothing bags and there is no law against traveling with cash so it was to be returned immediately. The SO pleads with the judge that it is part of his case in establishing intent to distribute, and the judge's response was, 'Don't make me tell you again!'

"So, even way back then, they made it hard for us to do our jobs, and it has only gotten harder and harder over the years!"

Soup ends his story as the guys sitting around start shaking their heads.

It isn't like in the movies. This shit is real, and it is rarely fair.

CHAPTER 1

OPPRESSIVE HEAT

The heat coming off the ninety-foot cliff in front of me is suffocating, I have to force air into my lungs, much like breathing through a gas mask.

The *whoomph–whoomph–whoomph* of the helicopter rotor blades beating the hot afternoon air just off to the south is a secondary thought in my mind. We mount up into the three-vehicle convoy and speed forward, Primary in place, heading just a short distance up the gravel roadway to the next stop. The Primary will dismount and head inside the location for his meeting while the rest of us all stand around in the hot sun awaiting his return.

His four-man team moves off with him in a perfect diamond-shaped pattern, plates on, protecting his every move. If a hit is going to come, it will be in these moments of movement from the vehicle to the building and back. This is the most exposed time for the Principal/Client/Diplomat or whomever you are escorting.

On rare days I could almost hope to be the driver—at least he sits in the vehicle with the AC controls on full, waiting for the "go" command to move to the next location.

Did I say it was hot? I mean *killer* hot—104 degrees hot—in full kit. The plates are ceramic, not metal, but that only makes them lighter—not cooler. A nearby rock wall is reflecting the sun right back onto each of us, standing guard outside of the transports. We stay occupied scanning, checking for threats, looking at buildings, huts, other vehicles, cars, and sandy rocky outcroppings for any movement or activity that seems out of place.

I am in the lead vehicle, designated Vehicle One. Vehicle Two is where all the Cool Guys ride—the AIC (agent in charge) and the package man. No one can touch or speak to the Principal/Package. The AIC rides in the front passenger seat of the vehicle, providing navigation and team communication. The Principal rides in the back seat, behind the AIC. Then the tactical commander, or TC—who is the door man for the Principal—stays with the vehicle to get the door on the return of the Principal. Then the Shift Leader, the "control guy," releases the Principal, floats, and commands the diamond formation.

It is not the most exciting work in the world of armed security, but you do get to run full kit, with primary and secondary platforms hanging off your body. Most times we wear suits or blazers or light jackets and do our best to hide all our gear under them. Sometimes, if the threat is high, like today, we run out in the open to show any potential threats that we are hardened targets ready to fight.

Gavin de Becker wrote a great book on security—*Just 2 Seconds: Using Time and Space to Defeat Assassins*. The book covers a lot of past assassinations and failed assassinations. The author includes journal excerpts and interviews with the killers, describing in full detail the failures or wins for the security teams. A number of great examples outline how a well-armed, tough-looking team have acted as a clear deterrent for assassins at all levels of society, even up to recent presidents. Just looking the part has an effect. It's a book worth reading.

And when you talk about thin-slicing a second or two of time, I have personally participated in training that outlines the effects of "he who moves first, wins." Two people face each other—one the adversary, the other the victim. They stand six feet apart. The victim turns and runs away as fast as possible. The adversary is not permitted to move until they see the victim move—then they can give chase. Amazing how this one-second space and time gap predicts survival. Have the adversary move first and almost always the victim is captured.

As we bake in the sun, Sean—aka T-1—is standing thirty feet away, off the other front vehicle's corner, looking forward and right, over the expansive open areas toward the tree-lined rock face a few hundred yards off.

Sean shouts over, "I am so hot I am not even sweating!" I respond with, "You are dehydrating is why—drink more Powerade when we get back in the ride."

The next words out of his mouth are, "Contact right, RPG!" as a rocket-propelled grenade streaks in, just missing the hood of the vehicle, overshooting it by a foot to hit relatively harmlessly in the dirt thirty yards beyond—just short of the building the Principal is in. Thankfully, RPGs are much harder to shoot with accuracy from a few hundred yards away than Hollywood would have you believe.

The shock wave from the explosion pushes through us, disrupting the blood–brain barrier to form small brain lesions, which lead to traumatic brain injury, often known by its acronym, TBI. The blast disrupts our thoughts for a brief moment as the shock and realization of being attacked sets in.

Enemy fire starts coming from my forward ten o'clock position up in a rocky outcropping, rounds snicking and screaming past me to strike Vehicle One in the driver's side windshield and the engine and cooling system.

Going to ground, prone out, to make myself as small a target as I can, I return fire at the direction of the muzzle flashes and rising dust.

Hearing T-1 returning fire on the RPG position, I sure as hell hope he is able to take them out before more rounds come in. It will not take a direct hit to fuck this day up and cause a lot of problems.

Despite my hope, another RPG comes streaking in, leaving a white trail in its wake. This round is much higher than the last, aimed at the building and not the convoy. The explosive round strikes ten feet to the right of the main doorway, ripping a hole in the side of the building.

As my carbine empties, I scream "Black!," knowing I can't possibly be heard over the noise of the firefight, but training habits concerning an empty gun stay with you. Tactically, when one's platform runs dry it is better to transition to the next, in this case my handgun. However, I really need the superior stopping power and accuracy of my carbine if I plan to eliminate this threat in front of me.

Rolling slightly on my hip, I can easily reach a fresh mag from the chest rig attached over my ceramic plates. Dumping the spent mag to my left with a slight wrist-flick, I set the fresh mag and drop the bolt. Ready to fire, I roll over twice to my left in order to have a new position and to potentially gain a better angle on the hiding place of my shooter.

My radio crackles to life. "Bravo Team, Alpha Team is coming out with Principal, moving toward the vehicle for immediate exfil! Shut those threats down *now*!"

Jumping to my feet, I run toward the threat at a left angle, slicing the pie at speed. It is quiet behind me, no sound from T-1. I send some suppressive fire into the rocky outcropping as I move, keeping my head down as I move for cover. I slide in behind some rocks and T-1 grinds in right behind me, ripping the leg of his pants across his knee. Blood starts to flow in the heat of the day due to his elevated heart rate, but we both know it is just a surface wound and nothing to worry about.

Two guns to one, we communicate the Bounding Left Drill, and, as T-1 lays down suppressive fire, I am up and running. In my head I hear my old firearms instructor, Predator 03, say, "I am up, moving, he sees me, I am down." As I slide into the next bit of concealment, I immediately put rounds into the rocky formation, as T-1 completes the same run I did, though he pushes past me a few yards for a better tactical advantage.

Over the radio I hear "Moving!"—the Package is out the doorway as the diamond closes tight around him, "plates on," sprinting for the Suburban.

With Vehicle One out of commission—dead driver, engine shot to shit—Car Three moves forward on the inside to provide concealment to the moving team, and if possible, to jerk out and become the lead vehicle.

T-1 and I are far enough left that I start the push forward, up the grade to the pile of rock that hides our bad guy. He is only occasionally able to get rounds off due to our heavy return of fire. I am "black" again, and drop my carbine on the sling and draw my handgun as I dive headfirst behind rocks so small that I am still heavily exposed. Sucks to be me!

Sharp pain stitches my right leg, thigh, and side as rounds strike just under my protective plates, and other rounds splatter the dirt and gravel around me. Our assassin must have changed position so he could send direct fire right into me. I send a few more rounds from my handgun as the realization of death sets in.

T-1 is up and moving fast, pushing past me, seeing I am hit hard, sending hate at the new location of our threat. I hear a cry of pain and surprise followed by more rounds as T-1 makes the hard corner and continues to pour rounds into the threat. "Threat down!" he calls over the radio.

Rolling over to sit up, I hear the gravel crunching as he comes back to my position, the convoy of two vehicles racing off in the distance about a half mile away, a dust cloud forming around them, the disabled lead vehicle sitting a hundred yards away.

Standing over me, he says, "It sucks to die my friend." In reply I quote my tag line from my Law Enforcement Training Foundation: "Training … the only place you can die all day long, in order to live on … Forever!"

We both laugh as he helps me to my feet. The Suburbans are turning around and heading back toward us. The radio crackles. "ENDEX, ENDEX, ENDEX, exercise is over, all to rally point for debrief."

It does suck to die, but you learn so much from the experience that it is difficult to frame the thoughts into words. Training is the only way to improve, learn, and understand.

Our assassin comes out from hiding, bitching up a storm for how many rounds T-1 slammed into him from his Sim Carbine. The RPG's shooter—aka Face—crosses the floor of this 2,000-acre gravel pit we train in, with its ninety-foot rock walls on three sides. For fake RPGs they do get your blood going when they come screaming in. Good thing he missed that Suburban or our field training officer would be pissed—it's his everyday ride! I could just see a broken side window or big dent in the side...

Face is an absolute stud. You meet a bunch of them in law enforcement and armed security. Oh, for sure there are many who don't take care of themselves and get lazy and fat as fuck, but the ones who come out to train are fierce and strong, stuffing their bodies into what we call *shmedium*-sized shirts, so their bulging muscles will show.

Face got his tag because of the 1980s TV show, *The A-Team*. Just like the actor Dirk Benedict, this dude has style, rocking a $600 haircut that is sharp enough to cut you if you touch it! Face rolls around in a white 1970s Corvette, and loves his Walther PPQ. There could not be a more fly guy in the bunch. The only sad part is that he is so young he at first did not know who Face even was!

That gives you some insight into how fucking old I am.

Tiger Lily is one of the vehicle drivers, a short, compact character. I can't figure out how he hides a full-sized handgun inside his waistband. He always has a knife in one pocket and a flashlight in the other, and is a lover of the M-1 Carbine and the Ruger Mini-14. You can't understand unless you're part of this culture, but his uniqueness causes him to fit right in. We train a lot together when he is in town. He often stays at my guest house. He does a lot of out-of-town jobs—security and protection details mostly.

We roll out to the pavilion for the after-action debrief, hot-washing the details and learning how to work as a team. The goal? To live as long as possible.

It is pretty easy to be a bad guy. They kill their fair share on first contact. Learning to react to contact and work as a team is the only sure way to achieve success repeatedly. We discuss methods to protect the driver of the lead vehicle. Having an up-armored vehicle would keep him alive long enough to get off the X.

We own armored vehicles and use them when active threats or high-value items or people are transported. Armored vehicles have their own unique challenges and limitations, like cost of maintenance. Rifle-rated armor also tends to limit speed and mobility.

We review the thinking that went into the team moving the Principal from concealment in a building to open skies with active threats and incoming fire.

It increased risk to the Principal, causing me to take aggressive offensive action to displace a threat that did not have an angle on the Principal and could have been suppressed. Plus, I got shot to hell and T-1 ripped his pants!

Their view is that such a small building space would not withstand a direct RPG hit, so they had an overwhelming desire to get off the "X."

The brass always seems to win, while we are bleeding out and dying.

After the group review, I review how I could have lived longer—better choice of cover/concealment, rate of return fire, and use of smoke for added cover.

But sometimes it's just bad timing that gets you killed.

CHAPTER 2

RAJ AND THE DRUG DEALER, PART ONE

Rajesh Nambootri Nimbalkar, or, as he urges his American friends to call him, Raj, hands change for the fifty-dollar bill a customer just gave him back through the Plexiglas window of the Q-Mart Drive Thru his family owns.

As the car drives out of the beverage tunnel, he lifts the tray from the register, sliding the fifty-dollar bill onto a stack of other large bills he has obtained throughout the evening, selling beer, wine, "loose cigarettes," rolling papers, and other items their customers need to keep their fix going in life.

Raj used to share the responsibility of running "The Tunnel" with his dad, but since his father died, it's now all on him. His mom works the inside for gas and walk-in customers and his mom's brother comes by often to check on them and help when deliveries come in and need to be put away.

It is not an exciting job, but they have a lot of regulars Raj's family has gotten to know through the years. His family seems to make enough to live on—his parents sent him to the best local college for an MBA so he can eventually get a better job than they did and help support the extended family.

Back home, there are lots of extended family to which his mom is consistently sending money. Some of his dad's family talk about coming over but never seem to be able to make the trip. Raj is never sure if it is money they need or the proper papers. His mom has always seemed skeptical of his father's family.

Whenever he can find the time, Raj plays the video game *Hunter Killer* with his dad's first cousin's oldest son Girish, who lives in India. The time difference can cause problems, like one of them sacrificing enough sleep, but the game is fun, and a welcome diversion. With his gaming headset, large TV monitor, and front-row seat for the live action, Raj always feels as though he is the first person in the game, killing bad guys all night long!

The biggest issue in his life is whether Raj should take the job at the place he interned while completing his MBA or stay on at the store to help his mom. He can't see her trusting someone enough to hire them to handle the money, and her brother and his family all have good jobs and no time to be working here.

Raj slides his vibrating smartphone from his front pocket to see a text from Girish. "I so need to come over to America and hang out with you!" This was becoming a constant thing with Girish, always wanting to come to America to visit. Raj keeps telling him to "get on a plane and come on over. We would have a blast together!"

When Raj told his mom about Girish's constant texting, she was skeptical about him coming over. She said she did not think he had the papers and passport to do so. Raj never asked Girish about those things—he just wanted to connect with his family. He had not seen Girish in five years, since his parents and he had been back home for the funeral of his father's mother, Raj's *nānī*.

Raj's father, Jalaj, had stayed a few weeks longer to help settle the estate, sending Raj and his mother home to take care of the store, which had been closed for a week while they were gone. His parents would not let anyone *ever* help them with the store.

Pushing aside his complex thoughts about his future, Raj looks up as the next vehicle—a late '90s green-and-primer-grey Z28 Chevy Camaro—drives into The Tunnel. It's not the cleanest Camaro Raj has ever seen. He wrinkles his nose as he's hit with an all-too-familiar smell filling The Tunnel.

The Camaro is leaking oil.

The driver is younger than Raj by a few years. He's going to have to card this dude. "What can I get for you?" he asks the kid ... Well, not really a kid, but still young.

"Hey ... can I have a twelve-pack of Fat Tire, and half a dozen loosies?," which is slang for loose cigarettes.

"Listen, my man ... I need some ID before I can bring those out to you."

The kid passes the ID like he has been doing this all day long. Examining the card, Raj sees a photo of the young, long-haired blond kid staring back at him. "Okay ... Chance Richardson ... I got you coming right up."

As Raj fills the order, the kid says, "My friends call me 'Take a Chance.'" Laughing at his joke, he asks, "What's your name, bro?"

"My friends call me Raj." As he hands the beer and loosies into the open driver's-side window, Raj sees Take a Chance pass them to another guy about his age in the passenger seat.

"Too bad those loosies aren't the real deal, huh?" Chance says, shaking his head.

"What do you mean?" Raj answers. "They are real tobacco."

Chance laughs. "No, no. I mean, too bad you don't have any *weed* in them. That's what we called them in Detroit when I lived up there. Dudes would sell us loosies, but they were joints! And some good shit too!"

Raj shrugs. "Sorry, man ... nothing like that here in Ohio."

Leaning out the window and smiling, Chance says, "I could hook you up. You could make some real cash-and-carry, my man!" He hands a bunch of bills to Raj, who walks into the booth to make change. As Raj slides his hands over the bills to put them in the drawer, he notices that one feels thick. *Heavy*. He brings it up to his face and checks it out. Chance sees him and asks, "What's up bro? You don't like my cash?"

Keeping his eyes on the bill, Raj knows it doesn't feel right. He handles cash all day long. He knows what a bill should feel like.

Chance again smiles. "Well, damn man, just give it back...I can give you another."

Raj answers, "I am supposed to keep these and turn them in."

"Aww come on, don't make a deal out of it...Just let me change it up for you, no hassle."

Raj responds, "Sure thing, Chance. I don't really want to deal with it anyhow." They exchange bills and Raj finishes making change. As Chance pulls away, he says, "Remember. I can hook you up on some good Detroit loosies! Be seeing you, bro!"

...

Once the Camaro makes a left turn out of The Tunnel and rolls to a stop at the light, Chance says to the kid in the passenger seat, "I told you that would be a hard pass. That money don't feel right."

Chance absently rubs the pea-sized lump on the left side of his forehead where a slug sits just under the surface of the skin. The hospital would not remove it because he does not have any insurance and it would not have any negative impact medically, but damn, it was a true reminder of how closely death can stalk a man.

The slug was from a pot deal gone bad. Sitting in an apartment building parking lot in Niles, waiting on a girl to pick up some bud, Chance had his head buried in his phone, texting his next stop, and out from around one of the buildings the girl's brother stepped, AR-15 in hand, firing a round through the front windshield, just missing Chance's face. Raising his head from his phone, Chance turned the car around to get away from his attacker, who put eight more rounds all the way around the car.

As Chance was speeding away, a round ricocheted off the trunk, cutting a long, deep furrow into the metal, smashing through the rear windshield, and the rear headrest, into the back of Chance's headrest, and into the back of his head, where it traveled around his thick skull to the left side of his forehead.

Chance rubbed it often, and, when wildly hammered, he toyed with a knife, wanting to cut it out. But deep down, he just didn't have the nerve.

Anyone who knew guns and tactics could clearly tell the shooter had no clue how to use an AR-15 effectively, or he would have dumped twenty rounds through the front windshield in seconds, decimating everything in their path.

CHAPTER 3

AIRPORT EP RUN

I just love the high rate of speed that traffic moves down I-376 heading toward the Pittsburgh International Airport. Sure beats that run in the opposite direction to Cleveland International! The Rt. 480 and Rt. 271 interchange is always a mess with a glut of cars and daily accidents. The Pitt trip is slightly longer but makes for an easy day of travel!

For today's client I am nothing more than an armed chauffeur. There is no credible threat against himself or his family, but, having known him for twenty years, he likes the personal service our security company provides in getting him to and from the airports.

Allen's family are third-generation apartment complex owners. It's a high-end complex, with a swimming pool, tennis courts, huge oversized units ... It costs top dollar to rent their places. No need to be a slum lord to make a profit—these guys have been doing it right for decades and enjoying the benefits all the same.

It is great to know high net worth people, people who still work for their money and understand the value of it. People who constantly give back to their community and employees. It helps me feel like there is goodness in the world after all.

I can see a big storm rolling in from the west as I cruise down the interstate—thunderheads reaching way into the sky with the sun reflecting off them like cotton balls, the bottoms of the clouds jet black, with lightning bolts dropping out of the bottom, angrily striking the earth!

I pull the dark blue Tahoe up to the "Arrival" portion of the airport, below grade, and pull in at the very front of the line, and back in close to the vehicle behind me. I am sure he is bitching at me about crowding him, but no way am I making my client and his wife walk two hundred yards with luggage to the end of the line.

I am up on the curb in my soft grey suit, crisp white shirt with no tie, and black shoes with a high shine on them. It is obvious to anyone looking down the line that I'm the chauffeur for some big-wig dude coming home. I scan the vehicles and people sitting around and smoking, getting a read on things, making sure no one is agitated about my choice of parking spots at the head of the line.

Once planted on the curb, I send a message to the client: "This is Trevor McCowen from Atlas Security Corp. I am here for your pickup, parked outside of baggage claim. Take a right out the doors." I was early and did not expect an immediate response. I cooled my jets on the curb, getting stares from people walking by. This part of the world does not see many "drivers" or "security" people.

Beyond my parking location is a lot for deliveries. I watch as a young man pushes a cart of food and water up the walkway toward the double doors. Doing a normal threat assessment on him, my educated guess is that he's on his way to resupply some food vendors inside the terminal—nothing squirrely at all. Back to watching the people coming and going ... and waiting. Something you get to do is a lot of waiting. Oftentimes it's hurry up and wait!

My phone buzzes on my side with a text message. The client is "waiting to offload the plane, something about the threat of lightning and they can't let us deplane."

Fifteen minutes later, a police officer walks up the line of cars asking people to move off. When he gets to me, I wait for him to repeat his message. "The storm is keeping them from unloading the luggage ... going to be at least twenty minutes. I would like for you to wait in short-term parking, please." I thank him for the information and text the client that I'll be back around and to inform me of when he and his wife get to baggage claim.

If they don't get this plane and luggage worked out soon, I am going to be late for my next client pickup! I have never had an issue like this at the airport.

Pulling into the airport gas station, I use the bathroom. I pick up some caramel popcorn in a box and a fresh coffee. This gives me permission to sit in the parking lot and wait versus fighting through traffic for parking in the big lot.

Fifteen minutes later, mine is the only vehicle in line at the baggage claim location. The officer is two hundred yards down the line, sitting in his cruiser. I step up on the curb and text the client my location, and stand stoically surveying everyone around me.

Allen, my client, informs me they are still waiting on their bags to be offloaded. They were told they could just leave and come back later to pick them up, but they really want their stuff and to just go home. After forty-five minutes of waiting, I notify Control that I am going to be late to the next client pickup and to please contact them and make them aware of how sorry we are.

Sometime later, I see my client and his wife exit the baggage claim area. I move to open the back hatch of the Tahoe and take their luggage to load it. Allen apologizes for making me wait so long for their luggage. Listen ... when it comes to clients, never let them see you sweat or worry about anything. You are just happy that they are back in town and ready to go home.

Merging into traffic, I keep to the speed limit. It is never appropriate to speed or drive recklessly. The few moments that you may save can cost you an accident or the embarrassment of a ticket in front of the client.

The client's health, safety, and comfort are your only concerns.

CHAPTER 4
THE DAILY GRIND INTERRUPTED

The range of emotions going through my brain makes it difficult to concentrate on the mundane tasks of my day job. The adrenaline is still high in the bloodstream, even the day after training hard at Close Quarter Battle.

The stack of client folders and reports in front of me was mind-numbing. Rebalancing investment models, moving assets to cover client distributions, writing buy and sell orders, updating beneficiaries, and writing reports does not provide the same level of excitement I get from the gentle recoil of my suppressed AR-15, chambered in 9 mm, pushing empties out of the way for fresh rounds to slide into the receiver. Or the lightly heard clink of brass striking the gravel at my feet as I take a corner, sweeping my carbine across my lane of fire, searching for a threat to engage. How can a stack of forms compare with tracking my partner from the corner of my eye as he sweeps his sector, using hand signals to stack up, and pushing through the next closed doorway with speed, the violence of action, and—when needed—overwhelming fire power?

It can't.

But here's my dilemma: As much as those fast-paced activities haunt my days and nights, I still need to concentrate on the nine-hundred-plus investment clients that I serve on a daily basis. My life is full of client meetings, discussing people's financial goals and objectives for retirement, planning for college educations, and ensuring the paying of mortgages. And everyone wants a beach house in a place where the sun always shines. At the end of the day, this is a job that requires more psychology skills than math skills.

I sit in meeting after meeting, day after day, with clients that talk about how analytical they are in their investment planning, how they carefully do "the math" to determine if a choice or decision is right for them, when in reality they simply make overblown emotional choices based on want, greed, and fear. And it is my job to manage their expectations and craft an investment plan to fit inside of that emotional wreck or they will simply get frustrated and go to another broker and start the process over again, buying into the market when it is at a high and selling out when fear drives them crazy and the markets are at a low.

Pulling me out of my thoughts, my cell phone lets out an abrupt chirp combined with a faster than usual vibration. Even on silent, my phone will emit an audible sound when a certain special text message comes into it. Then, regardless of what I am doing, I drop whatever it is and answer the call.

Snatching the phone from my side like a Old West gunfighter, I punch the security screen with my fingerprint to unlock the encrypted text message from my team leader, the owner of Atlas International Security Corporation, the man with the $600 haircut that is always cool and stylish. The dude never wears a hat and no one ever uses his given name. Everyone calls him by his handle—"Face." It must be hell being so pretty. And not Fabio pretty, but *GQ* stud-muffin pretty.

Atlas is a fairly new security company, designed to work insurance fraud, executive protection and valuable transport, alarm drops, and more. Primarily, we seem to get jobs protecting wealthy people's property when they travel and, strangely enough—funerals.

Those are not bad gigs, as work goes, sitting in a driveway for half a day in a marked security company cruiser.

Because of this type of irregular work, we all have day jobs and fill in when the work is available. There are a large number of guys with White Cards (the Ohio Armed Security Identification Card) working for Atlas Corp. Many guys hold jobs at local police departments, SWAT agencies, and there are even a few Drug Enforcement Agency studs who enjoy these interesting side jobs. There are also some non–law enforcement guys as well, like me. I'm an investment planner. There's also a computer tech guy and a plumber—not to be confused with a "pipe hitter," which means a member of the U.S. Special Forces. Absolutely no one wants to stand in a bank for eight hours a day, or ride in a coin truck delivering money to stores and, the worst of all, manning a gatehouse post at a factory. We do what we must to hold us over till the next Cool Guy job.

The training needed to obtain armed security certification with the Ohio Peace Officer Training Commission—provided by the office of the Ohio attorney general—is not overly difficult. First, you need the classroom study, understanding rules and laws and what duties you are permitted to perform and learning the nomenclature of various firearms and proper handling, loading, and unloading of each style of firearm.

The shooting portion comes next, which is very similar to what members of law enforcement undergo annually for requalification. Once this is all complete, it is really just the beginning of your education. Your agency then implements *their* training program, which you must complete and pass—normally a series of push-ups, sit-ups, and a mile and a half run—all timed and scored. This is not something guys can do cold; most everyone needs a few weeks of practice to get these all done in the time allotted.

There are classes for use of force, and for using tools like handcuffs for detaining people, a baton, and oleoresin capsicum (OC) spray. It's always a good time being sprayed in the face with Mace and having to perform various tasks with this OC jell dripping down your face, choking off your airway, making you think that your face is *actually melting off.*

One of the more exciting classes is driving. Everyone runs through this training. You are taught convoying, vehicle shielding, evasion, spinout recovery, J turnouts, and a lot more. At the end of the multiday training session, the best drivers are assigned their role—their primary function then becomes that one task. Drivers drive, and they are required to do that shit well.

If your agency is good, they will teach you other valuable lessons: Vehicle Stops and Approaches, Building Search, Subject Control, and a host of medical Self Aid and Buddy Aid trainings. I even have my K-9 CPR certification.

For me, there is nothing like following the hinge of a door that has just been breached by the number four man ... Crossing the threshold, dynamically passing through the "fatal funnel," checking my near corner, rotating my hips, turning toward the room, covering my lane of fire, locking down any targets in my sector, and, through it all, *breathing.* Don't ever forget to just breathe, and to communicate with your team.

Now that you have a better understanding of the training we all undergo, let's get back to the text message. I can see that it's a Team Communication— everyone in my training command is being notified of this information, meaning the radio operator at command central, the medic (who is also a gun-totting badass), as well as the drivers, who also carry secondary weapons and fill out roles when needed. Every security officer who is available is expected to respond to this message.

The text message summons is for *immediate action, come as you are: callout to Rally Point HQ.* End of text message.

I am twenty-five minutes from Atlas Corp. headquarters in normal traffic, but this is midday, which means it's going to take me a little longer. As my mind considers the three basic routes of travel I can take to my destination, I am packing my appointment book and other important papers into my shoulder bag. From my closet I grab my Go Bag, with my full kit—ballistic helmet, gloves, black pants, shirts, and head covering—and my modified gym bag that holds my folding-stock 12-gauge shotgun and multiple types of rounds, from slugs, Double 00 Buck, to Less Than Lethal bean bag rounds and pepper rounds.

I would love to be hauling around my sexy little AR-15, chambered in 9 mm, with the skeletal folding stock and suppressor, but Ohio has no certification for anything other than handgun and shotgun for armed security.

Actually, you can carry anything you wish. However, if you use it in a deadly force encounter you had better be able to articulate the need, prior training experience, and relevance to that particular situation, so prosecutors can determine if excessive force was used.

For Team Jobs like this one, I stick with state-certified platforms. However, when I work as a singleton, I carry the AR-15 platform for the extra round count, fire power, and speed of reload.

Plus, that platform's carry bag is discreet-looking. It's shaped like a tennis racket.

With both hands full, I move quickly down the short hallway from my office. Using my butt cheek to press down on the large door handle, I shout to my two secretaries, Noel and SAM (SAM is the nickname she uses, made up of her initials—something about her dad wanting a boy), "I got called up! I'm rolling out. Reschedule my 4:30 client meeting for another day!" The anticipation of the callout is almost too much for my mind to get a grip on.

I hear a weak response from my staff that they have it covered as the door closes behind me. It's great to have dedicated staff that care about our clients and the extra work that I do on the side. They really bring it all together.

I slam the door to my F-150, buckle up, and turn on the team radio, even though I am a bit too far out of range to pick anything up. I turn on a second radio with the local law-enforcement frequencies programmed in to listen to what is happening around me. I slide the truck into drive, feed gas through the pedal, and roll out of the parking lot, heading toward the four-lane a few hundred yards away, hoping to make good time with the flow of traffic.

The truck radio is locked, as usual, onto a local jazz station: Rick Braun is currently hammering out his cool, smooth tunes with his custom-designed trumpet.

I am eight miles per hour over the posted speed limit on Route 80, heading west. State highway patrol and the City of Girard monitor these few miles of interstate, collecting fines for speeding, overweight vehicles, and other infractions. Because it's an interstate that passes through New York City and over to Chicago, it's a path for drug runners.

As Rick finishes a tune with a run of soulful notes, the local law-enforcement radio crackles to life: "312 to Radio."

The local prefix for the department is the number 3, followed by the officer's badge number. I do not spend enough time in this town to know who this particular officer is, but I have trained with a large number of guys from different departments in the county and may know him if I saw him.

Radio dispatch comes back: "Go ahead, 312."

"I am In Service and Code 35." Meaning he just came on shift and is on patrol. I look in my mirrors and up ahead at the turnout, to be sure he is not sitting there with radar in hand ready for the afternoon race everyone seems to be on in life.

It's a very fast twenty-five minutes to HQ; my mind is full of all the potential reasons to call up the team. I try to keep my mind calm and focused, but it's no use. The thought of violence of action is constant. And because it's constant, does that make it a worry or a fear? Every sane man thinks and plans, knowing that every plan is useless at "first contact," but the planning is what brings success to a mission.

As I park, I am relieved to see other guys exiting their wide range of vehicles, turnout bags in hand, heading for the main building to change and get briefed on the situation.

A few minutes later, as we all stand around, coffees and energy drinks in hand, some guys still finishing up putting on plate carriers and straightening gear, the sound of stripping Velcro filling the room, Face (aka the Boss) begins the briefing: "A high-priority client is in a home invasion. We hold the alarm response contract and are to be the only ones who make entry. Local LE will secure the perimeter. The alarm company has an open panel mike and is feeding us live information."

Looking around the room, it occurs to me that I am the only one who is not a sworn officer. Armed security, yes ... but having a sworn commission does provide some benefits. My obligations and duties are to protect people and property from harm and end there.

We are just a few minutes from the property in question and it has been thirty minutes since the alarm drop.

The client and his family are in the upstairs master bedroom behind a locked door. So far no one has tried to breach the door, but it does sound like the vandals are smashing and grabbing what they can. Pretty brazen to perform an afternoon hit, and to take nearly half an hour to get your shit and get out. This is either dumbass kids, drugheads with no awareness of time, or professionals who know something specific is in the house and they are looking for it in earnest.

We will be using Alpha and Bravo Teams, four men to a team. We count off our numbers, and I am A-3, which I write on the underside of my forearm in marker. I don't want to forget this under the stress of engagement.

Because the client is safely tucked away in his room with his family, we will breach the front and back of the property and make our way to the client's bedroom to secure them. No hostile engagement if possible—our duty is to the client, his family, and that is it. His stuff can be replaced.

The guys who did not get drawn for entry duty will roll up and hold close perimeter, coordinating with local law enforcement.

Preliminaries done, we are out and en route.

With the local law-enforcement radio on for monitoring any progress, we are thirty seconds out when we hear:

"Radio, we have movement at the east side door."

"Copy."

"Radio, two subjects, loading stuff into a blue ford sedan."

"Copy."

"Radio, they are pulling out of the drive and heading west."

"Copy."

Well, fuck . . . they are getting away. Well, not really getting away . . . they are leaving the premises and that is good. Local LE will certainly catch these guys.

Atlas Corp. rolls into the drive, our two teams deploy, the extra man-power takes up perimeter and we breach the front and back doors like any other training or live mission.

The two teams work the rooms, searching for obvious danger but not clearing every potential hiding spot, keeping in mind the primary objective is to get to the clients, secure them, and then we can clear backwards out of the home.

Within minutes, we are knocking on the bedroom door, announcing our presence and confirming it is us with a cell phone call from Face.

The client lets us in and we secure his position and take stock of the family's well-being and overall heath—physical and emotional.

Alpha Team stays with the family and Bravo Team starts to clear the home in reverse order, starting upstairs, clearing all the rooms, closets, bathrooms, and attic, before moving downstairs to clear the main level, the basement, and the garage. This all takes about twenty minutes. The larger the home, the more rooms inside of rooms we get and the slower we move, checking under beds, and behind clothes in closets and drapes and so on.

As A-3, I am with the family, holding on the closed bedroom door, shotgun at low ready, eyes fixed forward, legs slightly spread, body weight forward, listening to the quiet conversation behind me, and concentrating on the team moving beyond the doorway. The team radio is silent. Face still has his local LE frequency on and turns the volume way down. The family does not need to hear the chase going on with the vandals who broke into their home.

Once we get the "All Clear" callout over the radio from the team, the perimeter guys move up to the house, and Bravo Team exits the home to hold position in the driveway. Alpha Team relaxes their body posture and we all started talking in low tones.

Face, as CEO of Atlas, leads the entire family through the house, telling them how Bravo Team checked everything—under the beds, in the closets and attic, and so on. His good looks and calm voice add reassurance to the family that all is safe and good.

There was no forced entry, so the perps must have come down the driveway, and in through the side door to the house that leads right into the kitchen area.

After the family is calmly back in the kitchen area, Face talks to the client about the habit of locking doors when home, even in the daytime. He advises him to consider adding some cameras to his security package. After the client readily agrees, Face lets him know he'll have the alarm company we refer work to come out to help assess the placement of the units.

We also work with a local insurance damage agency—they are really fine craftsman builders who clean up after storms or floods and repair fire damage. Face makes a call on the spot, asking them to come out to the home ASAP to assist with the cleanup of the mess made by the intrusion.

After being on-site about an hour, we mount up to head back to Atlas HQ for the debrief and after-action hot wash.

CHAPTER 5
WALL OF ODOR

The client currently sitting in my office—let's call him Tony—is a retired medical doctor who took care of me and my family for years. We were so close that often he would stop at my house on his way home from his medical practice and treat us. Such service and friendship you cannot find anyplace today.

He and his nurse wife got tired of the insurance racket in healthcare, became increasingly jaded, and left one practice after another. The trouble is, once you have spent so much of your time and money getting to be a doctor, how can you just leave it after only fifteen years?

He told me a story of an uncle on his mother's side of the family, a total drunk, who hung around the VFW all the time, hated the government, but fiercely loved his country and his flag. He would scoff at parades with veterans in them, making fun of them as they passed.

"After he died," Tony continued, "some people from the government showed up at my mother's house. After coffee was served and small talk dispensed with, the older of the two men reached down into a large shopping-type bag and pulled out a beautiful wooden box with a glass lid insert. Beyond the glass were medals and ribbons. He set the box in the middle of the table and opened it. My mother and I were not sure what we were looking at, so I asked them whose medals these were.

"The younger of the two cleared his throat and said, 'They were your brother's, ma'am. He was a highly decorated veteran of WWII.' The shock on my mom's face and the torrent of tears that followed were tragic to see. 'How could this be?' she asked. 'He never spoke of his service other than to say how much he hated it and what a joke it all was.'

"The younger man continued with, 'Your brother was a specialist in the service, attached to the Office of Strategic Services, known as the OSS—a precursor to the present-day Central Intelligence Agency.' There was silence for a long time. I looked up from the box of medals and said to the men, 'What did he do for the OSS during WWII?'

"'We don't have all of his records, but you can see that there is a Purple Heart, along with a Bronze Star for heroic service and various campaign metals.'

"I pressed a little harder. 'No. I mean, *what* did he do in the OSS?'

"The older one said, 'It says in the file that his specialty was Close-in Knife Work.' Then there's this very long pause, followed by, 'You can image what that would be like back then.' My mother's sobs got louder."

Tony looks up from his hands as they lay in his lap, sitting across from my conference table, his wife sitting quietly at his side, and says, "That's when I knew what I have to do. I have to join the Army and serve my country."

I look at him with wide-open eyes and say, "But there is no way! You are well over forty years old, there is no way they would take you!"

Tony shakes his head. "They need medical people. The Gulf War has made it hard to find doctors and they are taking about anyone they can find. I've sold my medical practice. Mary will go to work at the hospital. My contract is six months in-country and six months home."

"Holy shit, Tony," I said, after collecting my thoughts a moment. "I don't know if I should cry for you or hug you out of pride for your choice to join!" Big tears were rolling down Mary's cheeks. She knew this was truly his choice and she was not going to stand in his way regardless of the personal sacrifice she would be making.

Now, let's fast-forward a decade. Same office, same conference room table, only this time Tony pushes his chair way back into the corner of the room so he can sit with his back to the corner so he can watch the door and the window.

I look over at Mary, who laughs and shakes her head and says, "This is how he is now."

Tony interjects with, "PTSD is real and it seems that I struggle with it."

I have seen them a few times over the past ten years. Mary and I ran into each other once in the mall at Christmastime. We sat on a bench and she caught me up on how everyone was doing. I could tell it was hard for her to be alone with just her son when Tony was away for so long.

They would use little codes so she would know what country he was in. If the beer was good, he was in Germany. If it was wine, he was in France. Oftentimes, however, there was nothing to distinguish his location.

Tony's time in the Army is finally up. At his current age, it is a physical challenge for Tony to complete the requirements of his service contract. Old injuries and mishaps, along with his advancing years, have taken their toll on his body. Like his uncle, he too has a few of those medals. Campaign medals—Kosovo, Afghanistan, Iraq. Meritorious Service Medal. Combat Action Medal. And a Silver Star, along with his lieutenant colonel silver leaf uniform pin and patch.

Tony scoffs at the above-mentioned medals, much like his uncle did. What mattered most to him were the countless acts of selfless service he had provided to the local people in the places where he was stationed. The awards he treasured most were not from the military. They were instead in the most human of forms—small tokens or handmade gifts from the locals he treated—kids mostly. These are the things that touch the soul and warm one's heart, because they provide a little hope for humanity.

I remember one story he told me some years ago when he was on his six-month rotation home. He was assigned to a six-man team of very special operators. He was so excited to train and work with these men, who looked at him as an equal, even though he was twice their age, that he became the Number One on the door, meaning that, after the door or wall is breached and a nine-banger is thrown into the room, Tony was the first man through!

This went on until one of the smarter ones on this elite team realized that their medic was the guy they needed most of all, and they were letting him take the most risk! That put an end to a wildly fun time in his career. From then on, he was relegated to the back of the bus.

Another time, he talked about how hard they had worked in this area and had another mission to run late in the night, and he was just exhausted. He laid down to sleep, and his six-man team held security for him as he lay there resting. That is brotherhood at its finest.

There was another story he told me about being in the Kosovo campaign during the Yugoslav Wars. I don't remember if he ever mentioned the exact year, but I'm thinking it was 1995. Ironically, I had met another ex-military guy on the shooting range six or seven years ago, Keith Burrows, early winter 2014, I believe. Keith is a happy-looking guy who works for the next county over's Sheriff's Department. He always has a slight smile on his lips, not quite a smirk, but something else, like he is telling jokes... About *you*... in his head... and enjoying his own commentary.

His mustache reminds me of the cop shows, or classic porn, from the 1980s. Of course, he would have only been about ten years old at that time, but cop shows can leave a lifelong impression on kids. Makes me wonder what his favorite TV show was... *Miami Vice? Starsky & Hutch?* Old *Adam-12* reruns? Or mayber *Crime Story* with Dennis Farina! That dude had a killer 'stache!

Keith dresses efficient and neat but well out of style, like so many of the military guys do that served in the late 1990s. The guys today that get out of the service all seem to go to Buckle to buy their jeans and graphic T-shirts, looking cool and hip, working the ladies. The guys from the '90s, on the other hand, seem to have given up on style and keep wearing the Levi's and Wranglers, and solid-color Ts tucked into their jeans with wide leather belts with large buckles, a very retro style, but not yet classic. Some think it's a self-created style all its own, but the truth is, they just don't give a fuck what anyone thinks of them. I figure having to wear military dress for so many years kicks some of the flash and dash of modern society out of you.

I am guessing he is about ten years younger than I am, perhaps a little more, but at this age, it doesn't really matter. We relate well enough. After all, we are both standing under a tarp pulled tight with 550 cord, keeping the snow off us, listening to the crunch of gravel under our boots, as we watch guys down range ringing steel targets with handguns and AR platforms. We each have a handful of lemon-filled cookies in one hand and a cup of coffee in the other.

Slung over his shoulder is an old-school M-16, complete with the full plastic stock, in 5.56 mm with a 20" barrel. Maximum firing range 3,600 meters, effective firing range 550 meters. This one was a Colt, complete with the third-position selector oftentimes referred to as the "giggle switch" or fully auto selector. Once you fired this weapon on fully auto, you were sure to giggle like a school girl with glee!

Standing there in the cold air, I pull a quarter from my pocket, a clean hole through the center, the metal material mushroomed out the back side, holding it out for him to inspect.

"308?" he asks.

"Yup, at 300 meters."

"Very nice. Were you in?"

"Not me. When I was eighteen years old, I could not handle my dad telling me what to do, let alone some drill sergeant at 4 am."

He laughs. "Well, that is true enough."

"It took me until ten years ago to mature enough to let my wife finish an entire sentence."

"I don't have that issue," Keith says. "I have never been married." Changing the subject, he asks, "So how many times did you shoot at that quarter before you hit it?"

"Five or six times," I grunt.

He says, "Just be glad that quarter was not shooting back. That tends to change your focus a bit."

"Where did you deploy?" I ask.

Keith looks at me, like *Do I really need to tell this asshat anything about myself? Shit ... he already broke the cardinal rule with his question about my service.* "Bosnia," he says.

"GeeZus! My medical doctor served there! He told me stories about the mass graves. His exact words were, 'Have you ever seen ... have you ever smelled a mass grave?'"

Keith flips out his cell phone and starts to scroll through images of his current life, until he gets far enough back that it seems like a time capsule has been opened. He is much younger, standing beside a teammate, M-16 with 40 mm launcher affixed to the underside, looking sternly at the camera, a two-story stone home in the background partially destroyed by heavy fighting. This is all well before the days of Selfie Madness. This is much more like documenting something.

The next photo is of bleached white skulls, in small piles, mixed with white-grey rocks. Lots and lots of skulls and many more rocks, which resemble the skulls and add to the shock of what I am actually seeing.

Keith says, "If he said *fresh* graves, he was there well before me. These are older bones. It was near the end of my deployment. 1997." I asked what his mission was. "Hearts and minds ... winning over the hearts and minds of the people." He continues with more images, more mass graves and destroyed homes, and a photo of their base—a large stone home they had fortified for their use.

What a wild regional war that was ... Serbian forces were accused of mass-murdering ethnic Albanian villagers. Some 700,000 Albanians were driven from their homes and country. Of the 237,800 homes in the region, over 92,000 were destroyed completely or heavily damaged.

I wondered if it came easy for him to reveal these inner thoughts from years ago, or if my questions somehow caused him to leak out his pain ... Like

I poked a hole in a water balloon and the stream of water arched out and fell to the ground. It seemed that he needed to speak about it.

I remember the story Tony told me about his experience in the Kosovo campaign. Again, he was sitting in my office and asked me, "Have you ever seen a mass grave?" He shook his head as if to get the memory rattled into place. "No, no ... have you ever *smelled* a mass grave?"

"Ah, no," I answered. "The worst thing I ever smelled was a dead cow that had died giving birth. I was hunting groundhogs on a local farm, and the odor was like a physical wall keeping me back."

Tony nodded. "You are right about the 'wall of odor' being almost physical. Now multiply what you experienced by tenfold. Dozens of bodies ... these were people, families with lives that mattered, just gone, reduced to a heap in a pit, all their colored clothing haphazardly meshed together."

Total silence filled my office space. I looked at Tony's wife. Her eyes were fixed, staring out the window, her face wet from tears. How the hell could I say anything to affect that massive amount of pain? After a moment's reflection, God laid these words in my mouth: "How many children did you help and heal?" A half-crooked smile appeared on Tony's face, although a faraway look was set in his eyes.

"Kids ... children really. They follow you everyplace you go. They want to talk to us, to hear us speak, and to hear about what it is like back home in the USA. Most had no living relatives. Refugee kids. I often wonder what became of them ... I have them frozen in time, like a memory stuck solid. I want to know that it mattered, what we did ... That it at least mattered to these kids. The government would not permit you to give away any of your issued gear or clothing to locals, but I could give my nonmilitary-issue clothes, T-shirts, socks, sweatshirts, and candy to them." He said that he had left more clothes around the globe that are on the backs of poor, starving, sick people than he could count. "These are the most rewarding awards to have," he repeated. "But even time will erase most of those memories of service."

The last story he told that held specific significance to my understanding of the wars he has been through was when he was stationed at Abu Ghraib in Iraq. How it was broken up into different sections—one for the Army's use, one for the CIA's use, and so on.

Mary interjects. "Tony was very down during this period. He hated being in that place. It was a dark time for him. Everyone knew what was going on, but no one had the authority to stop any of it. He became very depressed, and as a medical doctor he was often called on to treat the prisoners."

When the base he was at, Camp Redemption, was attacked on April 2, 2005, with mortars, rockets, RPGs, and smalls arms fire, as well as vehicle-borne IEDs used to try and breach the wall, it was wildly chaotic. He didn't elaborate too much on the attack, but I read about it and was amazed at the jeopardy the base was in. At one point, ammo had run so low in one defensive position that the men were ordered to affix bayonets to repel insurgents.

For a guy raised in a small town, who only wanted to become a doctor to help his local people, Tony sure had seen the world. His service changed him drastically, but somehow fulfilled something deep inside of him. It is a great honor to meet these people and to learn of their life and stories.

One of my clients, retired now, was a C-130 pilot. He once spoke about his service, on how they were fired upon with RPG, SAM, small arms, and AAA during fifty percent of his missions. Twice fire trucks met his plane upon landing to put out fires.

There are people and companies who are trying to honor these men and women and their service and sacrifice. Lots of documentary movies are being made about specific actions of men and companies. Real stories—not the Hollywood fictional action we have all been raised with.

I have found that there is no single way to express to all of them how you feel. Many scoff at the "Thank you for your service" statement. I just try to be there, present, and ready to help or to ask if I can help. None of them are good at taking help and none want to feel less-than.

I relate the Abu Ghraib story to Keith that Tony had told me. Keith is very familiar with it. I tell him they should make a movie out of it.

Keith says, "I don't think we need any more movies about war. Seems to be enough said, don't you think?"

Well, actually, no, I think. *There is much more to be said.* But I don't wish to insult him, so I change the subject back to the shooting competition we were watching, which is not a money shoot, but an ego shoot. A couple of sheriff's deputies are battling it out with handguns to see who can hit a fourteen-inch plate of AR500 steel from the farthest distance. So far, that distance is 300 meters with a 45 acp. The holdover was 20 feet high and three foot for wind. The spotter was using his sniper rifle scope to call out hits and walk the shooter into the target.

Ranger, aka Eric, is very proud of his shooting skills.

We all have to be proud of something, right?

CHAPTER 6

SMALL TOWN/SNIPER TOWER

The town in which I work is small—3,800 people and one traffic light. Two banks, three pizza parlors, four convenience stores, couple of bars, a laundromat, a barbershop ...

I'm sure you get the picture.

Five miles in every direction is some other town, some larger ones, with plazas, movie theaters, restaurants, and specialty shops. Some of the others are smaller, with just a few hundred people controlled by a few stop signs.

But if you were from here and not just rolling through to or from work, everyone would know you. That's how it is in small towns.

I have worked in this community since 1991. Prior to that, I was in a small "city" with 6,800 folks. Still lots and lots of agriculture in the area. Everyone with any land at all rented it out to be planted with corn, soybeans, or winter wheat. A few old, dying apple orchards could be found and a lot of roadside produce stands.

The town I live in is 14 miles away through one traffic light and two stop signs. It is smaller than here, just under 2,000 people. We have a town circle or square or Green or Glen, depending on who you are. The Apple Pageant is held every fall with a large parade.

My place is 100 acres, 30 in crops, 35 in timber, and the balance in second-growth scrub brush and old pasture that is low and too wet to do anything with. The creek that runs through the place a half mile back is the real reason I bought the place. Well ... that and the barn, which is more than 100 years old.

A few years back, I had built a set of stairs, with a platform and snipers' nest, for long-distance shooting. Here I was, up high enough to shoot over the hills and crops. I also built 14-foot-high dirt mounds as bullet stops and placed 18-inch by 36-inch steel plate at 100-yard intervals out to 1,000 yards for some first-class long-distance shooting.

I have three distance rifles, each for different purposes, with different "glass" on them—an AR-10, AR-15, and a bolt gun in the new sexy 6.5 Creedmoor caliber with big glass on it—for the really far shots.

It is a rather relaxing and enjoyable way to spend an afternoon, lying prone on a platform, tucked out of sight in the deep shadows of the overhanging roofline of the old granary, watching the wind in close and through the glass out far. Watching the heat waves of the mirage dance across the fields.

Locating your target—perhaps the steel full man–sized target half exposed from the corner of the Shoothouse, some 700 yards away. Adjusting for elevation, holding off for the 3-mile-an-hour wind, slightly moving leaves on the trees about a half a milliradian. Relaxing the breathing, finger in the trigger well, feeling the slight movement of the release lever in the shoe of the trigger as your finger adds pressure … This platform I am holding has been adjusted to a four-pound pull. Concentrating on the crosshairs rising and falling with my heartbeat, I mentally tell my finger to *gently* add pressure.

I am already heavily loaded up on the by-pod, my support hand squeezing the sandbag under the butt stock for the slightest increase in elevation.

As the trigger breaks and the shot is away, I hear the reduced recoil through the suppressor. The added weight keeps barrel jump to a minimum, and I catch a glimpse of the bullet trace as it arches the nine foot of drop over 700 yards. I see the splat of the round on the stark white target, and wait for the clear *ting* of steel as the sound carries back. A very clean center-mass hit. I work the bolt, ticking in for another round to send down range.

Can I talk the technical talk of a sniper? You've just read a demonstration. Can I shoot a rifle? Yes, I can shoot a rifle—even over a long distance. But do these make me a sniper? Sweet Baby GeeZus … NO!

If you ever get to know a true military sniper, you will learn that being able to shoot well is the easiest part of the work. Being able to carry large amounts of gear, undetected, through difficult terrain, in wildly nasty weather, in order to gather intelligence, for a long period of time, when you are tired, cold, wet, and miserable—these are the qualities of a sniper.

All else is just play.

CHAPTER 7

RAJ AND THE DRUG DEALER, PART TWO

Rajesh Nambootri Nimbalkar, who goes by Raj, watches as the old, partially restored, green and primer-grey Camaro pulls into the drive-through
line of Raj's family's Q-Mart—nicknamed The Tunnel. Good ol' Chance
Richardson was coming by for the "re-up" of pot Raj needed in order to keep
the customers happy in their new *joint* venture. They loved that "funny-
punny," as Raj called it.

Especially when they were stoned.

Although "Take a Chance" Richardson grew up in Detroit, he had been in
this Ohio town long enough to know his way around. He lived on Washington
Street SW—not the worst part of town, but struggling just the same.

Raj and his mother live in Howland, a much nicer area, close to the mall
and lots of stores and restaurants.

Chance had recently picked up a house from the city that had been taken
for back taxes well after the last financial crisis. He paid ten grand for it. *Cash.*
Because Chance, although young, had already learned a couple of valuable
lessons. First, cash is king and gets people's attention and, second, real estate
does not abide by the IRS $10,000 reporting of cash transactions as banks are
required to do.

As an up-and-coming middle-man drug dealer, he was doing alright.

Wishing the driver of the car just ahead of him a good day, Raj waves
Chance up a little farther so their transaction will not show up on the security
camera. Raj had adjusted the one camera in The Tunnel so that it only got the
roof of the car and not the front windshield, through which you could see the
transaction taking place.

Smiling, Chance hands Raj a brown paper bag with seven ounces of pot in
it. In return, Raj hands back a bag containing a four-pack of energy drinks and
$1,500 in mixed bills, to cover Chance's costs for the seven ounces. Without
looking in the bag, Chance fires back his standard response: "The math had
better be right!"

Raj nods and says, "It's good man, just like always. If something is wrong,
just come back around."

As I told you when I initially introduced the players in this *joint* venture, Raj started out selling loose cigarettes—not legal, but not a large
enough crime to get pinched for. He called them "loosies." The guy does
love a pun! Chance then suggested they start selling loosies, but with a little

adjustment—instead of cigarettes, they'd sell joints. If Colorado could get $15 per joint for prescription-grade, they should be able to get $20 a stick for good, old-fashioned quality weed.

The math is sort of crazy—grams, ounces, and pounds don't all mix together proper—but they just make sure the excess profits land in their pockets.

Raj knew that Chance had to pay less for his larger buys at quantity, but it's not a felony to have seven ounces of pot on you. Raj couldn't get busted with a felony, and that was all that mattered. If he did, he would be dead...I mean *really* dead—D-E-A-D—no mercy from his mom and her brother.

Raj paid about $230 an ounce, depending on the quality. He rarely smoked it, so he left that determination up to Chance (but not up to *chance*: yet another of his funny-punnies).

So, the math: $3,700 for a pound makes about 290 sticks. Sell those at $20 apiece and you're netting $2,100 per pound.

So far, they were not selling a ton of it, but that's still some decent extra cash. Since Raj's father had died, his *amma* (Indian for mother) needed all the business they could get to make a living and keep the store.

Lying in bed late at night, exhausted, Raj would think, *What about* my needs, *amma? I also have wants. I need a cool car like Chance's, nicer clothes, shoes, a necklace...maybe even a girlfriend.*

On two different occasions, buyers had asked Raj if they could get larger quantities than he could sell them, so he and Chance had worked out a plan. Raj would have them wait down the side street at an empty gravel parking lot, and Chance would roll up and take care of them. He even passed on a little finder's fee to Raj for brokering these deals.

Raj knew Chance had to be paying no more than $2,500 a pound. He had taken the time to thoroughly research street pricing. But, as long as he made his money, Raj couldn't care less how much his partner made.

As an extra layer of security, everyone buying loosies had to buy some-thing else as well. Raj didn't care what it was, but he had to show sales to his *amma* and uncle for all the traffic coming through.

Most of the people that came through The Tunnel were on their way home from work. They bought mostly beer, wine, or energy drinks, and things like chips, cigarettes, and lottery tickets. But, more and more, Raj was getting high school and college kids rolling through The Tunnel at all hours, asking, "Got any loosies man?" And Raj would hook them up.

These school kids, rolling around with daddy's money, always bought three to five sticks. Any excuse for a party, Raj figured. Some of the girls riding with these rich kids were incredibly beautiful—nothing like Indian girls. Very slender hips and small breasts. Golden-colored hair seemed to be all they ever had.

By this time, Raj had a good pile of cash hidden away. He was going to have to put some in the bank. Next time he took a deposit for the Q-Mart, he would look at opening an account for himself. His parents always had a lot of cash around, whether it was from the store or maybe they were not claiming it all on their taxes ... Raj didn't know. He had learned about accounting and tax methods getting his MBA. Sticking a stack of cash in his hiding place after a brisk night's business, Raj thought of something one of his professors always said: "The IRS only knows what you tell them."

If it was up to Raj, he would tell them very little.

CHAPTER 8
SEAN WATSON (TANGO-1)

At five feet, nine inches tall and 180 pounds, 33-year-old Sean Watson worked undercover narcotics in Detroit, Michigan. Fresh out of college, with a criminal justice degree and high hopes of making the world a better, safer place, he had joined the police force.

Ten years later, Officer Watson was growing soft in the middle from beer and pot, used strictly for medical reasons, due to prior injuries sustained from a car accident while on duty, when a drugged-out chick ran a stop sign at 80 miles an hour and T-boned his piece of shit undercover 1998 Jeep Cherokee. Never one for seatbelts, Sean was ejected from the vehicle, as was the women and the two dirtbags in her car. First responders did not know who belonged to whom, and with no identification on any of them, the medics collected the dead girl and the dead dirtbag, the mostly dead Sean, and the other, unharmed, dirtbag and sped them off to various hospitals. Sean should not have lived through the ten-minute ride through downtown traffic, but being one tough son of bitch, he did.

His multitude of injuries, combined with the stress of being married with children while working deep cover, made it easy for him to take a partial disability from the department and relocate to the north coast of rarely sunny northeast Ohio, to be closer to his wife's family.

Because of his premature graying hair, caused by the shock of that tragic car accident, he chose to keep his head shaved smooth. After a long stakeout, a stubble of three days' growth would show up—snow-white hair that caused him to looked much older than a guy in his 30s. His sad, deep green eyes reflected the violence and corruption of humankind. The only time you really saw the true man hidden inside the hardened shell was when he smiled, when his entire face lit up, and hope was restored to the world.

He was a quick learner and naturally skilled with tools of any kind, including firearms and knives. And let me not forget his God-given gift to talk bullshit like no one I have ever met. After watching him work a barroom of bikers and skanks over for drug intel one night in Detroit, his commander asked him to join the Cool Kid Club—undercover operations. Sean thought it would be exciting and meaningful, but that's all history now—long-ago war stories that few wish to hear. Give him a few beers and one or two tales will slip out and float around the room with all the other law-enforcement guys' current and retired stories of the past.

It was while working undercover that he learned how to "sneak and peek," as they say. The head of the drug task force would get a tip from someplace in the food chain—call-in from a disgruntled dealer, snitch looking to get a lighter sentence, or something fed down from the higher-ups—and Sean's three-man team would be given an address. No one ever discussed openly what their duties were, but it was whispered that they would break into the location and plant listening bugs and, if possible, video surveillance cameras, and stake the place out. Once they got credible information on the questionable subject, they would pass that back to the head of the task force who would then obtain the proper legal warrants to do what they had just done.

They would need to scrub all of the prior data so that the timestamp dates would coincide with the newly issued, all legal and pretty, warrant for surveillance. Then the real job began, as a new team would be tasked with the surveillance detail. Fresh eyes and new faces, in case a bad guy remembered seeing someone around too much.

It was during one of these "sneak and peak" operations that Sean got his handle, Tango-1. He entered the building through the front door, up the three flights of stairs in this crappy part of Detroit. They had seen the target occupant leave the premises and after three days of watching this asshole, they were confident the place was empty. After placing all of the proper equipment in the shithole of an apartment, Sean exited through the back staircase. As he made his way up the alley, he startled the number two man—the lookout who was watching the street—and new to this team, who hit his comms. Through his ear bud Sean heard, "Tango coming up the dark-as-fuck alley, may need to take this guy out, moving hot and aggressively." Sean, realizing it was him the number two guy was talking about, keyed his mike. "Hey dickhead! It's me in the alley … GeeZus … you need way more fucking training if you're going to be on any team of mine!" As Sean walked past the kid he muttered, "FNG!" It took the new kid days before someone finally told him FNG stood for Fucking New Guy.

He was butt hurt for weeks about it.

As the two men got into their dark-colored Ford, the drive quietly said, "Tango-1 down, Tango-1 down!"

Sean scowled. "What the fuck was that, Swanson?"

"Nothing, bro. Not a thing!"

But it stuck. All around the station Sean would hear the other guys say, "Tango-1," as he walked by. It then became commonly used during radio transmissions. "Tango-1, you are clear for insertion." Real high-power spy shit, but only if that kind of crap mattered to you.

Sean would later comment over beers how he felt more like the criminals they were chasing than the cops. All those B&Es to plant surveillance equipment can make one a little immune to the level of fear of being caught. Of course, if they *were* caught, their orders were to exfil, *immediately*, with as little damage and cause for alarm as possible. Nobody was to get rolled up and no serious pain should be caused to *anyone* on the street, period!

During these B&Es, the illegal ones, prior to the warrant, Sean picked up a crazy little habit of moving things in the location. Nothing big, but if a water glass was on the counter, assuming you could see the counter through all the dishes and trash, he would move it to the stove, or a hairbrush from the bathroom counter to the toilet seat (if there was one), or dump a pillow on the bedroom floor. Just some little thing to make the perp question his sanity. Considered unprofessional by definition, no one ever knew he did it.

Switching careers after the move to Ohio, Sean started working as a tech, running his own computer company, doing installations of hardware for homes and businesses, running cable and software programs for alarms systems and TV cameras, mostly to catch employees stealing from the till or checking on the kids to be sure they are not trashing the house while mommy and daddy work late in the suit and tie corporate world. This way, everyone gets to drive BMWs and go to private schools.

I met Sean at an indoor shooting range, roughly an hour and a half from each of our homes. We had both been driven indoors by the cold Ohio winter. I was just learning the shooting sport called International Defensive Pistol Association, and Sean was there for an interview of sorts. The club needed an NRA-certified range safety officer on-site for all of their practice matches and scored shoots.

Myself and an assistant prosecuting attorney from my county were gearing up for the Monday night event when I saw this bald guy with a scar on his forehead and missing teeth leave the circle of instructors and head our way.

I remember looking at him and thinking, "Man, if I was in a dark alley right now, this is the first motherfucker I am shooting!" He looked truly feral, like a fox or weasel bearing down on a mouse, and I was that mouse.

I took a breath as he walked up and said, "Hey. Nice Sig 226, but a striker fire will score better in this game. We are about to go hot as soon as the guys are good down range, so eyes and ears people!"

We've been buddies ever since.

CHAPTER 9
GUY FROM DUBAI

The economy has been a real struggle for many people in my area of Ohio. I have a number of investment clients who own their own businesses. After thirty-plus years of doing this, I have seen a lot of economic ups and downs, as well as clients age and children have no interest in the business that Mom and Dad built. Kind of reminds you of our guy Raj, right? Seems there is always someone closing up shop and selling a building.

We lost our General Motors plant a few years back. GM had been slowing production for years, buying employees out, transferring some to other locations. Their investment had been dwindling for years, and each of those years it seemed to have more and more of an effect on local small business.

Take today. I am on my way to a small town north of the city to meet a client who has held an auction and sold all of the contents of his family's plumbing business. There is a potential buyer for the building flying in next week from, of all places, Dubai.

Mr. Dubai is not a US citizen and is spending three thousand dollars on airfare to look at a building in a market that is becoming more depressed as the years go by. Why on Earth would this building, two blocks off Main Street, be desirable for a guy from Dubai?

Downtown is starting to look like a parking lot with all the old dilapidated buildings they have been tearing down. Now we are seeing plazas become empty and traffic lights removed. Many small communities are suffering the same way.

> Breaking me out of my lament, the radio crackled to life:
> *Brookfield Units, domestic, lock out at 912 Groove Ave.*
> *Car is running in the street, red Chevy*
> *Negative child in the vehicle*
> *Negative pet in vehicle*
> *Copy*

Turning the volume down a notch, I continue to think about Mr. Dubai. Of course I think nefarious thoughts about anyone who is not local. Especially someone from out of the country. What type of front will this be used for? I wish I could meet the guy and get a better understanding of who he is and try to read him as a person and feel him out for intent. But that's not why I'm being called in. In fact, my client couldn't care less what the guys intentions are—he just wants to get paid for the building and this guy happens to have the money.

I noticed the gas tank indicator light just came on, flashing on the dash, requiring me to push an OKAY button in order to clear the notice. Well, shit ... I normally fill my tank when it's just below half, but with the string of airport runs I've made this week, I didn't notice the gauge.

Atlas Corp. recently started an Executive Armed Driver Delivery service for clients wanting to be dropped off or picked up at the airport. It saves clients the hassle of parking nearly a mile away in the case of Pittsburgh or being forced to park off location and take a bus in the case of Cleveland.

We charge a lot more than what the cost is to keep your car parked at the airport for a week. However, you get curbside to front door service with the luxury of an armed driver/escort. No true need for the armed portion of the driver, no real known threats to deal with, but the world has gotten more and more dangerous and the violence seems to be increasingly random. Even with good conceal handgun laws in Ohio and Pennsylvania, most people still don't travel by air with their weapon, so having an armed driver for this hour and half drive each way seems rational.

I am passing through the old part of downtown, just a half dozen blocks from the courthouse, and roll into what use to be a BP gas station, but now has no name on the sign, although they kept BP's green and white colors. The hospital and doctor group are just across the block, and abandoned plazas and old storefronts go the entire block toward the old city center.

I roll up to a pump, and slide out, leaving it running. Once the door is closed, I lock it with the key fob in my overcoat pocket, walk around back, and prep the pump for filling the tank.

I am parked farthest from the building. People are walking in and out, paying cash for small amounts of fuel, and carrying cans of energy drinks and packs of cigarettes.

A dude comes out the door, over-exaggerating his strides, arms waving large, like Kid Rock, talking loudly, a clear plastic cup full of liquid in his hand. This is two in the afternoon, so it could easily be vodka. He yells over at me, "Nice ride, bro!" I nod my head but say nothing, not wanting to encourage him to wander over. My suit jacket flaps in the wind, and I'm hoping my handgun does not show beneath it.

Keeping an eye on discount Kid Rock, another equally sketchy guy is crossing through the center of the traffic light. I can see the tattoos on his face from where I am standing, thirty yards away. He is staring at my Tahoe as well, and I'm getting itchy about all of this attention.

One pump over, a car rolls up. A ratty-looking girl gets out, leaving her baby in the car seat in the back, heading in to pay for gas. She returns, pumping her five dollars' worth into her tank, after which she gets into her car, lights a cigarette, and pulls out.

Tattoo Face is now in the building, and the Kid Rock wannabe is standing out by the intersection and the empty sign, staring past me, between the rows of pumps. He then starts over my way, on the far side of my set of pumps, eyes locked forward, taking the same loping, arm-flinging steps as when I first saw him.

Fuck. This dude is going to come out around my gas pump and rob me! I think. *Shit ... how did this neighborhood turn to shit in just a few years?*

I am panicking a bit. I had not planned on getting robbed today. Wondering if I should draw on him, or give him what he wants, I continue to assess the situation. I have a protective vest on, but damn, there are still lots of spots to get shot in, assuming he has a gun.

He is now out of sight behind the pump that separates us. I place the pump nozzle into its slot with my right hand and rotate my body to the far side of the pump. I am now in a blind spot to the building, and no one can see me because I am between the vehicle and the pump. I drop my right hand to the grip of my handgun and wrap my fingers firmly around it. Two things happen in rapid succession—a car pulls up to the side of the pump from my blind spot in the road and wannabe Kid Rock flops into the front passenger seat. the car not even coming to a complete stop before pulling away.

My heart is pounding in my head from the spike of stress and adrenaline! Well, that was certainly wild. Not totally sure how I even feel about my reaction to this situation. Did I overreact? Could I have handled it differently? Was I really in any danger?

I don't even bother finishing filling the tank. I just close the cap and get back in my running vehicle.

Once I am back on the road, I can think about what occurred and try to come to an understanding of the situation.

A) I was aware of my surroundings.
B) I was reading the people and actions.
C) I was gauging the situation.
D) I was putting a plan in place.
E) I was ready to act if need be.
F) There were forces outside of my sight, playing into the situation I was not aware of.

And it would seem that I had subconsciously made the choice to fight versus giving up my money or falling victim to the possible unknowns of his attack. I was not going to start from behind the eight ball, but be ready to engage him as a threat.

Later, over dinner, I shared this story with my wife. She said that she is always ready to soak them in gasoline. The pump is high pressure and sprays a long distance, and no one wants to be covered in a flammable liquid!

Women ... always thinking. Men ... always doing.

We make a pretty good team.

CHAPTER 10

RAJ AND THE DRUG DEALER, PART THREE

The large, wall-mounted fan was oscillating on the High setting, trying to push air through The Tunnel as the sporadic line of cars came through to buy the "convince the relatives" items from the comfort of their cars.

All the fan was really doing was blowing the smell of burning motor oil from car exhausts into Rajesh "Raj" Nambootri Nimbalkar's face.

It had been just a couple of weeks and Raj had already sold pounds of pot through the The Tunnel. The loose joints, or "loosies," he was selling to customers for twenty bucks were really taking off.

At first it was just two or three customers a day—what looked like high school kids blowing daddy's money on two or three loosies at a time to now twice that many people rolling through The Tunnel looking to score. Raj had already sold a pound of pot this month, resulting in $2,100 of profit hidden away in his bedroom. If the present rate of sales kept up, he was going to need to start buying some new shoes, and clothes, and he still wanted a cool car like Chance's Camaro to drive around.

As he attended to the customers, Raj wondered what a sweet ride like that might cost.

Because the loosies customers had to buy something legitimate from The Tunnel—the "convince the relatives" items, Raj called them—when he sold them the pot, Tunnel sales had started to go up, thanks mostly to energy drinks, pop, gum, and beer, but still, any help in overall sales was important. Raj's mother had noticed and commented—in front of her nosy brother, Raj's uncle—how well he was doing in his own little space. He had to admit, he felt a sense of pride for helping the family make more money. He was beginning to think that maybe he should make the pot customers buy larger items when they bought their loosies. Maybe a $5.00 minimum? No more $2.00 gum. A few times, people had just handed Raj a couple of bucks and said, "Here ... buy whatever and keep it" and drove off with their loosies. He would slip that little extra into his pocket.

As another satisfied customer drove away, Raj saw Chance's green and primer-grey Camaro pull into the line for The Tunnel, reggae music blasting out of the after-market speakers. In the front passenger seat, Raj noticed a big, dark-colored man. His hair was unruly, not an afro, but going in every direction. As the man moved his head to the beat of the music, his hair moved like the waves of the ocean.

Raj waved Chance's car up a little more, so the camera—tilted as always to the roofline instead of into the windshield, as it should be—couldn't see who was inside. Stooping a little to look into the car and make eye contact with the dark man, Raj noticed that he looked older than Chance, with harder eyes, and a smile that looked practiced or fake. Chance turned down the music, causing the deep beats to fade and the passenger's hair to stop undulating.

"Hey Chance, what brings you through The Tunnel today?" Raj asked

Chance nodded his head toward the dark man. "This is Jean-Pierre Buteau. I just love saying his name ... Anyhow, he supplies me with the stuff you order. He wanted to get a look at the new wonder boy of loosie sales."

Jean-Pierre leaned forward, making eye contact with Raj. *"Bonswa.* Is dis true dat you sell bunch ah dese loosies a few sticks ev'ry time, brah?"

Raj couldn't help but wonder at this crazy-haired dude with a French name and an odd accent driving around in Chance's Camaro selling drugs in Ohio. But here Raj was, from India—not him, exactly, but his parents—running a Q-Mart in Ohio.

"Are you French?" Raj asked.

"Non, non, brah," Jean-Pierre said, his hair back in motion as he shook his head. "I am from 'aiti. Aftah de big earthquake in 2010 we moved tah Britain. I was ah boy ah ten who grew up in poverty. But America, brah, is de land of ... 'ow you say ... Milk an' 'Oney! Or maybe beer an' loosies!"

Chance and Jean-Pierre both laughed, as only two guys who are high and enjoying the moment can. Raj, wishing he was as high as they were, forced a laugh to be polite.

Abruptly stopping his laughter, Jean-Pierre again leaned forward, making a different sort of eye contact than his jovial greeting. He looked deadly serious. "Do not fuck this up, brah ... or all dat you know will end. All good things, yes? *Bon bagay,* as we say. Or else, *non bon bagay?* Dat be very bad." He held the cold stare longer than needed, wanting to make sure he was clear.

After a moment of uncomfortable silence, Chance let out a chuckle, breaking the spell. Jean-Pierre, again Mr. Friendly, slapped Chance's shoulder and roared with laughter. He motioned his hand forward, and turned up the tunes. The thick, heavy beat started to drift out the open window and his hair began moving with the sound as the Camaro rolled out of The Tunnel.

Raj stared after them, a little shaken by the threats—both in the words and hidden in the laughter.

Raj jumped as his uncle was suddenly speaking in his ear beside him. "Who was that?" he asked.

"Just some friends I met."

Staring at Raj for a moment with a look only slightly softer than Jean-Pierre's, his uncle whispered, "Be careful of the Haitians. They don't have *friends* . . . just people they can use."

As his uncle left The Tunnel, Raj noticed that his hands were shaking.

CHAPTER 11

A DAY AT THE OFFICE

The alarm panel chirps, alerting me that the front office door has opened. The automatic closer makes a small *thunk* as it recloses on the seal. I can hear some muffled conversation down the long hall as Noel, my assistant, talks to what sounds like someone with a whiney male voice.

I check my appointment book to verify that I don't have anyone scheduled for a meeting this morning. Nope ... just a paperwork morning for me. The voices stay low and I hear the alarm panel again as he opens the front door and leaves.

I hear Noel padding down the hallway. A moment later, she sticks her head in my open door, "Hey ... Soooo, that was Mark Claymen."

I respond with, "The guy who has the auto repair shop in Girard?"

"Yes, that's him. This is like the third time he has walked in over the past couple months to sign a distribution form."

"I noticed the trade requests for cash distributions. What's going on?"

"Well, this one was way stranger than he's ever been. After he signed the distribution form he said, 'Can't you just get me some money out of your big safe in the back?'" My eyes open wide. She continues with, 'No, Mr. Claymen, I tell him ... We don't keep money on the premises.' Then he says, 'Can't you get me some out of your purse?'"

I shake my head. "Damn! This guy has been a client for ten-plus years. Never once has he shown an inclination toward uncalled-for conversation or outlandish demands!"

Noel continues. "Then he says ... 'Pontiacs and prostitutes, some cost more than others ...' so I reached under the counter and got that big can of Bear Mace fog spray you got us, and flicked the safety off."

Because we are in a high-end, out-of-the-way location and never deal in cash, I have never armed my staff, never having felt the need in thirty years of doing business with the public. Now, with the rampant use of heroin and the casino not far away, people actually seem desperate!

Could this be what the Zombie Apocalypse looks like? Drug-crazed people we once knew and loved attacking us for money to buy more drugs, selling their girlfriends and wives for a bump of coke? My wife Sofia works with these people daily and tells me the most horrible stories at dinner.

I always thought it was a joke when the Centers for Disease Control issued their "How to" book on the "Zombie Apocalypse" because it had the same data you found in the book for hurricanes and tornados. I always thought it was a cool marketing ploy to get people, mostly young people or those who are fascinated by the series *The Walking Dead* to read something that would stick with them and actually help in a crisis. But who knows ... maybe not, maybe zombies are real, after all. Look at all the movies being made about killing zombies, even by President Lincoln and Jane Austen. I mean, really ... What the actual fuck is really going on in the world?

Noel continues with, "I pushed the form forward with my free hand and said, SIGN IT! And he scribbled his name and left."

"How much has he taken out over the past few months?" I ask. Noel gives me the number from a piece of paper in her hand. "That is more than half his account balance! What the hell is he spending it on?"

She says, "I think it's gambling at the casino, but today he seemed high on pills or something."

"That comment about prostitutes could be telling as well," I say. "Keep close track of his answers for why he is making distributions. If we feel he is being abused or someone is somehow taking advantage of him we need to alert the home office."

Noel gives a sharp nod of her head and pads back up the long hallway to her office.

I sit back, thinking about how much the area has changed over the last ten years. Heavy layoffs from the steel mills and manufacturing plants, GM closing their local facility, physicians prescribing Oxi like it's birth control, people hooked on all sorts of drugs, legal and illegal, desperate for the next high to keep them going ...

As I sit forward to continue writing an investment summary report for a client I think, *We are doing our part.* Sofia spent seven years in college getting her master's degree to council adults with addictions. I don't know how she does it. She has such great compassion and a true desire to help them. And she clearly knows that, first and foremost, they have to "want" the help and desire to get better. So many are in the program from Court Order Treatment Plans. Being forced to do something pretty much makes a drug addict or alcoholic a defiant five-year-old throwing a tantrum.

When she has a win, we celebrate together, but so very often at breakfast she reads the obits and finds a former patient that has OD'd. It is so hard to see them progress and improve and "coin out" of the program, just to get sucked back into the drugs because they could not totally change their environment. One of the many changes they need to make in their lives in order to have the best chance of recovery is to change who they hang out with, places they shop at, work at, whatever makes them think of that past life ... It's important to leave it far behind. Unfortunately, that may include a spouse who is oftentimes also an addict. And you simply cannot save them.

They must want to save themselves.

CHAPTER 12

POWER OUTAGE

WE DO NOT RISE
TO THE LEVEL OF OUR
EXPECTATIONS.

WE FALL TO THE
LEVEL OF
OUR TRAINING.

ARCHILOCHUS 650 BC

My eyes open to total silence and complete and utter darkness. There is always some type of illumination—the digital clock on the bedside, night-light in the bathroom, the sound of the hotel room mini-fridge keeping beers cold, the hotel furnace rumbling—all signs of the life of the building, but now, just nothing at all.

I sit up in bed and reach for my cell. It is 5 am. In the next bed, Sean (aka T-1) stirs and grunts something inaudible, then asks, "What is it?"

"No power."

Sean, never phased by Murphy's ability to screw up an easy job, says, "Well . . . fuck!" and sits up too.

I am immediately hit with that generalized anxiety that is caused when plans change last minute. The unknown path always jumbles my guts.

This layer of stress on top of meeting your deadlines just stacks on *another* layer of stress. And the *third* layer of stress is all the tasks you put off yesterday that you planned to do this morning before the job. Things like fill the gas tank of the vehicle. Yes, it has a quarter tank, that will take you 150 miles, or about two hours of drive time, but will it take you all the way to your destination, assuming you truly know where your destination is? Because you need to pick up the close follow in less than thirty minutes. Now the stations can't pump gas and you will need to wing it.

The hotel e-key is no longer going to work. We're going to need to prop the room door, the inner hallway door, and the outer building doors open as we transfer gear from the room to the vehicle. One man to move gear and one to stay with the room. We have to lock the vehicle each time—can't leave valuable equipment unattended, even if the parking lot is pitch black and no other soul is about.

There's still city water pressure, so I wash up and brush my teeth. Fuck . . . no coffee in the room! I eat a granola bar and wash it down with bottled water.

Sean is up and getting dressed. He then starts repacking his gear and computer, his flashlight—propped on his pillow—making strange monster shadows on the wall.

I head down the hall and outside to move the truck closer to the main door so our gear transfer will be easier.

It is dark. *Really dark*, no ambient light at all. There are just security lights over the doors of local businesses and a few cars on the road a half mile out. It's all very strange and eerie—the sort of shit you see when the world goes off the grid and ends. More anxiety is now added on. I don't want to be three hundred and fifty miles from home when the world ends—I want to be in my house, protecting my family.

I get into the vehicle and turn it over. Seeing again the quarter tank of fuel on the gauge, I curse myself for not stopping after I put our subject to bed at his hotel a half mile away. Not tucked in, but kept an eye on from afar until it was late enough to assume he was in for the duration of the night.

All I wanted was a bottle of water and bed after that long day of following him through Ohio and well into Upstate New York. The old saying comes through my mind: "Never put off... something or other." The truck windows are covered with heavy frost. I clean off the backup camera with my thumb, and put the defrost on high. I use the camera to back up as the vehicle heats and windows start to defrost.

The only available spot near the main door is the handicap space. I back into it anyhow. I keep the truck running and lock the doors using the keypad by the vehicle door handle.

Holding my pocket flashlight in my mouth as I haul gear in both hands down the long hallway, drool starts coming out of my mouth, running down the sides of my beard. The taste of aluminum combines with paint chips from the flashlight in my teeth. I push through the three propped-open doors, using my foot to be sure they do not close all the way and the rock holds them ajar so I can get back in.

As I reenter the room, Sean steps out and says he'll be right back. I recheck the last of my gear on my bed. Sean quickly returns with two Styrofoam cups of black coffee. Dude! I could not be happier! He says the big pot in the lobby was off but still felt hot, like the night manager made it before he left and before the morning guy came in.

Now that we are about to exit the building and get ready for the subject to trigger, Sean checks the local news on his phone.

"Power out in much of Waterloo, west side of Seneca Falls through Waterloo, and southern-most end of the county, effects 6,214 customers according to New York State Electric and Gas website. Use caution at intersections due to lights being out." He finishes reading the headlines and we move off, letting the door snick closed behind us.

Now to deal with the anxiety of looking for an operational gas station before we check on the follow subject at his hotel!

CHAPTER 13

RAJ AND THE DRUG DEALER, PART FOUR

Rajesh Nambootri Nimbalkar, or Raj to his friends, is walking across the street at the light, on his way from the Q-Mart to the bank up the block. In his backpack is $12,000 in small bills. He had sold about eight pounds of pot in the past three months through The Tunnel. He bought some new clothes and shoes, even a nice watch from Shinola, which are made in Michigan. He got the canary yellow Duck Watch for just under a thousand dollars. He loved how bright it was. Chance gave him a hard time about it. But it matched his new Adidas Ultra-boost DNA Sydney soccer shoes!

"Hi Mister Nimbalkar!" Bonnie the bank teller says, as he comes through the door. Few people can say his name correctly, but these tellers all get the accent correct. MacDowell Bank is one of the few remaining truly local banks in the area. Every year more and more of them are bought up by the Big Boys. Branches keep closing and people are forced to bank online or drive farther away for personal services.

Raj slides the backpack off his shoulder. Bonnie asks if he has another store deposit to make. "No. I have some money mother has paid me for working in the store I would like to put in my savings account."

Bonnie asks, "Doesn't she just write you a paycheck?"

"No. She said the accountant said this was easier and less of a hassle for our small location."

Bonnie asks another one of the "hidden" questions required for large cash transactions as Raj continues to take packets of bills from his backpack, laying them on the counter.

"What are you saving up for, Mister Nimbalkar?"

Not thinking much about the question, he says, "A cool car like my friend drives, but yellow!"

Bonnie notices the watch on his wrist. "You must like yellow! Your watch is pretty! Is it new?"

"I just got it last week and my new shoes came in the mail yesterday!" Raj says with excitement.

Bonnie and others had noticed his bright yellow shoes when he walked up the sidewalk past the bank's large window and entered the lobby. They were impossible to miss.

Bonnie's eyes get bigger and she glances over at the other tellers as Raj continues to build his piles of small bills.

"How much do you have there, Mister Nimbalkar?" Bonnie asks.

"Twelve thousand even."

Bonnie says, "Let me get the Currency Transaction Report form. It's required for all cash deposits over ten thousand."

Raj's head snaps up in surprise. "Ohhh ... really?"

"Yes. All transactions of cash over ten thousand dollars get reported, but it is nothing to be concerned about. You just write on the form what the cash is from. You can say it's your paychecks from work."

Raj says, "Never mind the form. I will just deposit nine thousand today. I have some more shopping I can do with the few thousand dollars."

As Raj starts putting some of the cash back into the backpack, Bonnie says, "Are you sure? That is a lot of money to be walking around with."

With a weak smile, Raj replies with, "It will not last long when I hit the mall!" All the tellers laugh.

Bonnie walks the large stack of small bills over to the counting machine and puts the first stack in. Once she is done with the count and hands Raj the deposit slip, he heads out the door with a "Thank you!" and thinks to himself, *I just dodged a big damned bullet! I am going to need to come in more often for these deposits so I don't have to file that cash form the teller was talking about.*

After Raj leaves the bank, his bright yellow sneakers glaring in the afternoon sun, Bonnie walks into the manager's office.

"What's up?" Theresa, the manager, asks.

"Raj Nimbalkar from the Q-Mart was just in and he tried to deposit twelve thousand dollars in cash. He claimed it was how his mother paid his salary. When I told him about the CTR form he balked and said he had changed his mind and only wanted to deposit nine thousand and was planning to spend the other three thousand soon!" <here>

Theresa says, "Really? I have never known them to be flush with cash. They always seem to pay their property taxes and other expenses on time, but never anything like that kind of extra."

Bonnie shakes her head. "It gets worse. Raj has been in three other times in the past few months and has deposited a few thousand dollars each time. I didn't give it any thought due to the small size of the deposits, but after what he tried to deposit today, it's definitely raising the red flag, as we say."

"Anything else I should know?"

"He had on brand-new high-end shoes and a high-end watch. It just seemed very out of the norm for him—or any of his family for that matter."

Theresa thanks Bonnie for the information. She brings up her computer screen and prints out the IRS Form 8300 called the Currency Transaction Report and enters in Raj's information and account number. Although the form is not required for deposits under ten thousand dollars in cash, it can be filed for any "suspicious" activity in an account. The nice part about filing the form for less than ten-thousand-dollar deposits is a copy is not required to be given to the customer.

The Bank Secrecy Act was there for a reason—to protect the banking industry from illegal money and from funding terrorist activity. Failure to report suspicious activity was a clear violation of her job as branch manager, and Theresa really likes her job. As she finishes the form and attaches it to an email, sending it up the chain of command inside of MacDowell Bank, she thinks about Raj and wonders what he could be mixed up in.

CHAPTER 14

FINCEN ENTERS THE STORY

I say slowly and with a measured tone, "I don't like the fact that you are using bribery—or the *veiled threat* of bribery—to motivate me. You do realize that you can gain a lot of information by simply asking someone to help? They will be far more helpful and faithful to your cause if it's their choice versus your *requirement*."

Over on my desk, my police-band radio squawks to life: "Control to Brookfield Units. I have an animal complaint."

An officer responds: "Go ahead, radio."

"61 Vineyard Street. I have a cat in the road."

"Copy. In route."

As the radio goes quiet, Mr. Philip Daniels shifts in his comfortable leather chair across from me, and I continue: "People don't like being *made* to do things. People generally want to help, to do good works, and to know that they matter in life."

I was on the verge of pissing my pants over this meeting. Thank God this guy from FinCEN just called yesterday to request a sit down. If I would have had to wait and think about this for a week or two, I'm sure I would have lost my mind with worry over what could be the meaning, purpose, or possibility of an infraction that I could have been involved in.

To be more factual about it, "this guy" stopped in last Friday, requesting to see me. My assistant Noel brought me his business card, which I saw was from the U.S. Department of Labor, with a gold shield stamped on it. "Mr. Philip Daniels, Investigator" it read, along with the 9th Street Cleveland Federal Building address. The last four digits of his phone number were scratched out and, in blue pen, four new numbers were written above the two lines of blue ink.

After examining it, I said, "Um ... I think this dude is a fake. He crosses out his phone number and hand writes a new one? Who does that? Did he say what he's looking for?"

Noel said, "Yes. He wants records on the labor union plan you manage."

"Well, now I *know* he's a fake! Never in all my years of working with unions have I ever had a DOL investigator come to me for anything. I think he's some local guy—maybe even a reporter—trying to get nonpublic information on one of our clients. Even if we do believe he's who he claims to be, we still can't give him what he's asking for."

"So, what do you want me to tell him?" Noel asked.

"Tell him, 'I think you are a fake and we are not able to help you. Here is our home office's phone number ... Feel free to call them and request whatever you want.'"

A few minutes later, I heard mumbling out front, followed by the main office door opening and closing. I looked up as Noel came back into my office. "Well, he is pissed! He was not happy at being called a fake! Then he jumps right into asking me questions about who the voting members are, and I tell him that I am simply not permitted to answer that question. Then he goes on to ask, 'Well, how would one go about taking money out of that plan if they so chose to?' and again I tell him, I am not able to answer that question. And he huffed, actually *huffed*, and walked out, all bitching and shit!"

The following Tuesday morning, the office line was ringing. Noel came on the intercom with, "Dave Honeycut from home office is on line one." I have met Dave a few times at the annual meetings of the five companies in our group. He is the top man at Compliance. Truly someone to be a little afraid of. Normally, one of his underlings calls to request we handle some client issue in a very specific manner or to request details on client assets being invested to be sure we know where the money is originating from.

"Hi Dave. How are you doing these days?" I said, with all the relaxed confidence that I could muster. I was holding my breath, awaiting his reply.

"I am good Trevor. You and the family enjoying life?"

As we got through all those little niceties we all use to set up a conversation, I was wracking my brain on what he could be calling about. Department heads just don't call field reps to pass the time of day.

Finally, I heard his tone of voice change as he shifted to a more professional level. "You had a visitor last Friday morning ... guy from the Department of Labor."

"Um ... yes I did," I stammered out.

Dave continued with, "Any reason home office was not informed of an investigation into one of your clients or why you called a federal employee a fraud and told him to leave?"

Shit. Fuck me!

Taking a breath, I kept my tone as even as possible. "Because the guy is lying to us for one thing, being arrogant with my staff for another, and even if he was being honest and is who he claims to be, I still can't help him. Any information he would be asking for must come from home office and we provided to him the home office phone number to call."

"Trevor... you do understand that you are required to help federal officials?"

"Yes. I am completely aware of my requirements, but there is no way I am going to break firm policy and procedure for some dude who rolls in off the street, unannounced, requesting information on a client, carrying a business card that has changes made to it with a blue pen!"

"Alright, alright—ease up a little. No one is burning you at the stake. But I will say that Philip Daniels is real. He does carry a Department of Labor business card, but that phone number he scratched out is his direct line to the Treasury Department in Cleveland. He's part of the Financial Crimes Enforcement Network—FinCEN." I could hear the excitement in Dave's voice as he spat out that last part.

Holy shit! What was the Treasury Department doing calling me about one of my union investment plans?

Back to the present, in my office.

The agent from FinCEN is all too happy to throw his power and authority around, now that he is sitting here face-to-face with me. After all, ever since 9/11 and the creation of the USA PATRIOT Act, federal agencies have been stomping all over the rights of people under the guise of justice and safety for all.

Title III of the PATRIOT Act addresses money laundering and expands the Bank Secrecy Act to encompass all financial intuitions, including life insurance companies, check-cashing companies, and many others.

FinCEN's mission is to "safeguard the financial system from illicit use and combat money laundering and promote national security through the collection, analysis, and dissemination of financial intelligence and strategic use of financial authorities." Or so the mission statement claims.

Section 326 of the Act (sometimes called the "know your customer" rule) makes it imperative that you have personal knowledge of your clients, starting with, but not limited to, their full legal name, address of residence, date of birth, and federal tax identification number.

So here this guy sits, being all threatening and bitchy regarding the "know your customer" rule and talking about "willful blindness." Telling me that, as the representative, I "should have known" this or that about the client, because, as stated in the manual, "You are the first line of defense against money laundering."

Get this—even if they cannot "prove" that you had knowledge of a client's intent or action performed with their own money, that you just happen to invest for them, FinCEN can still use their sweeping powers to smear you and actually *bar you from the industry* for doing business with someone who ends up on one of their many watch lists.

Just the veiled threat of being a pariah in your own beloved industry and unable to work again is enough to get people to fall in line with the federal government's goals.

The fines are twice the value of the laundered funds, up to $500,000. On top of that, they can hit you with twenty years in prison as the investment advisor! Hell ... the fucking *criminals* don't even get sentences that long!

We are sitting in my newly built office building, designed and drawn by myself, using the Craftsman Style of architecture and as many of Frank Lloyd Wright's ideas as I could jam into one space. As much as I love his architecture, I hate his furniture—simply no function to it. Instead, I complemented the clear maple woodwork and solid oak conference table with dark brown cloth chairs and soft tan leather appointments. The walls are painted in the color of Lion's Mane and the flat carpet has extra thick padding for a shoeless comfort my staff and I all enjoy—when clients are not in the building.

The guy leans back in my conference room chair and crosses his legs at the knee with a great show of confidence. I take a moment to look him over. Either they have a clothing budget or they are paying these guys way too much. This dude is wearing a beautiful dark blue, soft pinstriped suit, tailored in the current fashion and cut with the lapel at the current perfect angle so all his brethren can recognize his style and taste. The matching gold tie and highly polished black shoes and plain dark blue socks finish off his statement to society—he is elite and should be treated as such. The only thing missing is the pocket square, which I am sure is on his dresser at home, reserved for only high brass meetings ...

Over the past few years—with the inclusion of the annual DOL and Financial Advisor Regulatory Agency (FINRA) rule changes—the Fed has created and crafted a set of laws and rules that ensure that when they show up to inspect you as a financial representative, they will in fact find something that they can use against you as leverage to co-operate with whatever plan they have in mind for your client.

To defend yourself against a federal agency takes far more money, man hours, years of your life, and strength than most normal people have.

Don't get me wrong ... FinCEN does have a difficult job. It's not just the fear of terrorism but mobsters and tax evaders that all fall into their wheelhouse of duties. In 2016, a Nevada casino was charged with willfully laundering money by ignoring the anti–money laundering (AML) laws of the Bank Secrecy Act. That alone led to a $1,000,000 fine. You can imagine the laundry list of names that will come from following the trail of that money ...

When FinCEN sees money laundering through real estate purchases, they specifically require certain U.S. title insurance companies to identify the natural person or persons behind companies used to pay "all cash" for high-end residential real estate. It is easy to understand how flipping houses with cash deals can make dirty money clean again. In 2015 alone, 53% of all Miami-Dade Florida home sales were "cash deals," and there is no current requirement to follow the AML requirements for home sales!

Just within the past few years there was a case in Kentucky with a money services business, a Food Mart check-cashing company, which willfully and repeatedly violated the Bank Secrecy Act. The story goes that the Food Mart conducted $1,000,000 per month in check-cashing and money-order sales. The company's fines were due to their failure to file "timely and accurate" Currency Transaction Reports (CTRs), which *potentially* deprived law-enforcement agencies of valuable investigatory information. It was noted that one-third of the CTRs filed by the Food Mart were late and 95% of the CTRs were filed with incomplete or inaccurate information.

There are FinCEN cases of money laundering to Pakistani Taliban, multi-million-dollar bribery scams, credit-card scams, and tax fraud cases. In 2014, there were 14,000 tax-related entries alone!

The email fraud letters we all laugh about—"Your rich cousin from Pakistan wants to send you ..."—are real, as are unauthorized wire transfers, and thieves using your email and stolen investment account information to contact your broker or firm and request funds. The crooks are getting more and more bold and sophisticated.

I was not currently aware of which one of my hundreds of clients this guy was interested in, but to say that he had my attention was an understatement. After all, I have never had a complaint or infraction filed against me—and not because I am good at hiding things. I just find it far simpler to follow the rules, even if I do not always agree with them or understand the purpose for them.

Mr. Blue Suit—I am terrible with remembering names and I don't wish to look down at his calling card for the third time—reaches into the tan calfskin sling bag he has on the floor by his chair and retrieves a rather thin file folder.

Thinking it best to do so, I check his card for his first name again as he opens the flap of the file. Retrieving a 5 × 7 black and white photo of a dark skinned mid-20s guy—who looks really familiar—he slides it across the table at me.

"What am I looking at?" I ask.

The police ban radio squawks to life again:

"Radio … ah … yeah … this is 22 at Vineyard Street, I thought you said a *cat* in the road."

"No. *Calf* in the road, as in *baby cow*."

"Well … okay then. I must be at the right place!"

I personally would love to find out how this radio call ends, but, in deference to Mr. Blue Suit and the pissy look in his eyes at the interruption, I turn the volume all the way down.

Looking up from his business card, I commit his name, Philip Daniels, to memory.

"Do you know this man?" he asks.

Always feeling like I am being set up in a trap and not comfortable with the generalized word choices people use, I say, "Not off hand. I meet lots of people in my line of work. I don't recognize him as a client, but then again, I have clients I have never met, beneficiaries of deceased clients who live out of town."

That should cover it if he then pulls out some correspondence or photo of us standing near each other. I have no trust in this prick's intentions or helping him achieve his goal to trap me in a "lie to federal authorities," thereby forcing me to be his pawn in a game that gets him promoted and me out of a job.

"This guy is the son of Deepti Nimbalkar, who we know is a client of yours!" He pauses to let that sink in.

I raise my eyebrow a bit and say, "Okay, how can I help you?"

Mr. Daniels says, "Deepti Nimbalkar's son Raj has been in contact with people that have ties to radical believers in India. We would like to know any back story you have on the family."

"Raj, from the drive-through up the street? No way I believe that. As far as I have been told through conversations with his father, Jalaj, who I'm sure you know has now passed away ..." I let *that* sink in and watch his face for any sign of prior knowledge—sure enough, he already knows the dude is dead. "... He, and now just his wife—Deepti—own a convenience store up the road. The whole family works in the store. I would see her a few times per year when I stopped in to see Raj's father for our meeting. A very pleasant women whom I enjoyed chatting with until he was done with customers and was available to meet."

Since Mr. Daniels seems interested in what I was saying, I continue. "She has been back to India at times to help her ninety-plus-year-old mother who still lives on the old family lands, which, from what Raj's father told me, total a fair amount. Her brother I have met a few times ... He seems to hang around the store enough that I see him when I am in. He oftentimes engages me in conversation, seems to really understand the markets and money. He has never shown concerns with market directions ... Not the normal panic from emotional people I am use to dealing with. It is my understanding that they are all very educated."

Mr. Daniels says, "Well then, if the family does not need you for your investment intellect, then they must be using you for something!"

"Hold on a minute," I reply, straining to hold my growing anger over where this is going in check. "Many people come to me for nothing more than a second opinion or some solid affirmations that the path they are on will in fact get them to the goals we have established. If this guy is somehow using me, he is doing it legally."

"Are you aware that Mr. Nimbalkar, whom, as you stated, is now deceased, had been sending money home to his brother's family?" Mr. Daniels spits out, a little too angrily. "And recently we have been alerted that the son, Rajesh, is also sending cash payments to his cousin Girish!"

"I have lots of clients who send money to family all around the world. There is no law against that. They use a checkbook attached to their investment account. But that has all changed now that Mrs. Nimbalkar has inherited his accounts and transferred them into her name with new account numbers and different banking instructions."

Mr. Daniels changes the subject from my clients back to the PATRIOT Act, chapter and verse: "You do understand that you are required to assist FinCEN with any investigation? It is written into the USA PATRIOT Act as well as in your contract with your broker/dealer."

"Bullshit!" I respond. "I could see how that rule applies if it is my *actual* client who is breaking rules and I am helping him, but no way can you force me to get involved in this through the extension of his family dealings with his son or widow and his brother-in-law living in India and *his* kid! What the hell ... you just looking to wrap *everyone* up?"

The prick starts from another angle. "We have had extensive conversations with your broker/dealer firm, and they are cooperating with us fully and would very much like you to do the same."

So, what in the hell could they be blackmailing my broker/dealer firm with in order to get them on board? Threat of a full-out audit? Shit ... maybe my firm just wants to help. They are required to help all federal agencies. Damn it ... I need to talk to some people before I break this level of trust with my clients. I need some solid verification that this is real and not just subjection to get me to play.

"How about you giving me the names of the people at my home office that you have spoken to about this so I can verify their willingness to push me out there on the pointy end of the stick to get roasted if this is all a bunch of BS and my client's family chooses to sue me?"

He produces a page with four names and positions on it: I recognize the name of the president of the company, having met him a number of times; the chief compliance officer—met him as well and of course just spoke to him about this meeting. The other two names I don't recognize, but their titles claim that they are responsible for the Legal Department and the Anti–Money Laundering Department. Shit! This might actually be a real thing. I don't know if I am terrified or excited!

I look up at Mr. Daniels, who says, "Look. This is the real deal. You said so yourself—'You get people to help by simply asking.' Well ... here I am, asking you to help me, help your government ... Hell, to help your country."

Well fuck! This asshole is good! I think I just may be all in.

After a moment's consideration, I answer, "Let me talk to home office and legal and get whatever documents I can have to protect myself in case I am violating some client rules or something. This is all a bit over my head, and I want to be sure that I am doing what is right and legal."

CHAPTER 15

INTERLUDE AT THE AIRPORT

Russ, my up-line manager from South Carolina and I are traveling from our home office back to the airport to head to our respective homes—he to North Carolina and me to Ohio—after our meeting with the four people from the FinCEN list that good old Philip Daniels provided. We discussed the AML case that FinCEN is working on concerning my deceased client, Mr. Nimbalkar.

Russ says, "Damn ... that meeting was not what I expected! I was thinking there would be resistance, but they are willing to give you anything to help out FinCEN. I can't believe the legal waivers they signed off on! I have been in this business thirty-plus years and have never seen anything like it!"

I could not agree more. "I am totally freaked out by it! Part of me wants to help and serve my firm and country, and the other part of me is terrified I am in over my head and only bad will come of this! And I really don't trust this Philip Daniels at all ... seems too gung-ho for me. I get the impression he will use me as a tool and discard me when he gets what he wants."

Russ, always being the optimist, says, "Brother, you are a stud, and will certainly stay ahead of this federal suit! I have no doubt you will bring this case home for him and walk away a hero!"

"Fat fucking chance that will happen, but thanks for the vote of confidence."

We grab some sushi at the airport, I know ... it doesn't sound like something you should do, but this truly is good stuff! We chat about our families and kids. His son plays on the PGA Tour and makes good money doing it. How wild it is to me that you can make hundreds of thousands from sponsors and purse money!

"My daughters are doing great," I say, always happy to brag about the family. "As you know, Keira is down in Wilmington working customer service with her boyfriend and Lilly is living in a rental house finishing up her master's degree in social work. She wants to work with children of trauma. I simply can't believe how big her heart is. To work primarily in the foster care system has to be heart wrenching and mind numbing." Not one to only share the positive, I add, "The guy she is living with is a meathead ... gym rat who claims to be a body builder. The dude is seriously big, but nothing compares to his ego and narcissistic lifestyle. Never was sure what my little girl sees in him."

Russ catches the check, and I dump the tip on the table—more than suggested, as is my habit—and we say our goodbyes, heading to two different terminals to catch our flights home. I am grateful for his steady hand working me through the corporate system and protecting me from management all these years.

These days, it's hard to find men of honor and integrity.

CHAPTER 16

PITTSBURGH AIRPORT CAFÉ

I am at the airport again! I always feel stressed until I get here. Always in a hurry, even if I am the recommended two hours prior to flight time. Inner stress is difficult to put down.

Travel days are always a bit melancholy. I am excited to be heading out to something new and potentially exciting, but I miss being with the family and taking care of my day-job clients and my hobby farm.

This particular trip is to St. Louis for more training. Specifically, the finer points of surveillance. Atlas Corp. is growing in the field of insurance investigation and we need to stay up to date on the finer points of *close follow* and overall surveillance of an individual.

The instructor of the course is a mountain of a man we have trained in executive protection with in the past. Ex-mil, Purple Heart, and owner of his own security company. They recently started a line of K-9 dogs for service. Some truly solid operators for sure!

Whew! Made it through security without a hitch and, this time, even managed to not piss off the TSA guys. It seems I always have one of those guys working me over extra good—hands in the waistband of my pants, patting down my legs and butt, using the security wand on me ... I had them find a paper clip in a pant hem once and another one in a suit coat pocket. I don't know TSA well enough to understand if they have a "flag system" for travelers, but I seem to have the word Target written all over me. My buddy Soup has a saying: "It's not gay if its TSA."

Don't get me wrong—TSA has a very difficult job. Last year they found 3,391 firearms in carry-on baggage across the country. That is a lot of forgetful people. But damn dude, going through my travel snacks and having your gloved hand in the crack of my ass as other tourists walk past is just no fun at all!

I can smell the coffee well before I see the airport café. The coffee-counter girls asks, as I approach, "What can we start for you today?" with the most pleasant voice. The glass case is full of banana walnut, blueberry, and chocolate muffins; lemon pound cake; and an assortment of cookies that look fresh and inviting. I confidently state my "medium coffee with cream" order and stammer over what delicious cookie and muffin to add to it. She smiles warmly and adds the walnut muffin and an oatmeal raisin cookie to a bag for me.

She is young, with short white hair, a hint of blue and pink still visible at the ends. "I like your fading color. My daughter rocks a two-tone blue!" I say, as I take my phone from my belt and sort through the images to show her a picture of my oldest daughter, mostly so she knows that I am not flirting with her.

"She had it dyed bright blue just after college and before her 'real adult' job as an account exec with Verizon, selling phone to corporate clientele." The young cashier looks impressed with the picture, and we chat about hair color as she warms up a piece of lemon pound cake and hands me my coffee in a large travel cup.

As I turn to the counter that holds the creamer, sugar, and lids, I notice "Green Pullover Dude" coming through the doorway. I yell over to him, "Hey man, we crossed paths again, you stalking me?"

The cashier wants in on this banter and says, "I can take care of him for you!" perhaps a little too eagerly.

I continue speaking to Green Pullover Dude. "I literally ran into you twice this morning." I give him a big grin, trying to be disarming after yelling across the room at him. No one else is in the place, but still his head shoots up when I confront him. He responds with, "Yeah, so what is it with that?"

The cashier adds, "Really, I got this if you need me too!"

I look at her and say, "If he shows up in Charlotte, we will certainly have an issue."

Green Pullover shrugs. "Naw man...you are good. I am heading elsewhere."

As I walk out the doorway into the growing bustle of the concourse, I hear the cashier say, "Okay, Stalker, what can I start for you today?" I snort and laugh loud enough that they both look my way. I throw a wave and continue on, my mind wandering to thoughts of her adding some exotic liquid to his coffee and taking him "out of the game!" But with her daughter's face tattooed on her arm and the Rosary tattooed around her other wrist I would doubt seriously if she was a hitter, but I found the thought amusing.

If this all was not strange enough, on my way through the giant airport parking lot earlier that morning, which covers a full mile from my vehicle in long-term parking to the gate, I passed a huge pickup truck. It was one of the oil field trucks—an F-450 all jacked up, covered in mud and black oil, with a big brown tarp in the back covering something that rose above the roofline of the cab. I could see a few cases of water in the bed, but no one around, although the engine was running. I stopped and considered my options. A peek in the driver's window did not show anyone slumped over in the seat, sleeping or passed out. The cab was empty. That tarp sure did look suspicious—was it hiding a fertilizer bomb, or just more cases of water? I couldn't image leaving your work truck in an airport parking lot (I was walking through short-term parking), closer to the main terminal, and not have your gear properly locked down and secure.

Well, I was not going to try the door, or lift that tarp...no way! Sometimes just being a good witness is enough. I took a photo of the vehicle, including the license plate, and the sign that had the parking-lot number on it. On my way to check my baggage, I stopped by the security booth and engaged the female officer. I explained what I saw and that I found it strange. She was thrilled I had a photo of the vehicle, the plate, and the exact location.

I never did find out if it was anything nefarious or just some guy who, in his panic to make his flight, left his keys in the ignition and his truck running.

One thing that I have learned, training with law enforcement these past five years, is that there are lots of very bad things that happen right in your neighborhood that are never reported and that you will never learn about.

Some of the law enforcement who train with me work in a small city just south of us that butts up against a larger city's bad part of town. One guy has pulled over and arrested seventeen guys who are felons with firearms in the vehicle! All for stupid infractions—no turn signal, broken tail light, and so on. Seventeen weapons in just eight months, and nothing at all reported in the news! That is just wild to me.

The news media claim that they don't want to concern the local residents about these types of arrests! What the actual fuck? People need to know, and not only that criminals are all around us, but that law enforcement is out there every day doing their part to keep society safe.

CHAPTER 17

COUSIN TALK, PART ONE

The gaming console cousins Raj and Girish used allowed them to communicate through text messaging in the comment section of the game they always played. Even though there was an eleven-hour time difference from Mumbai to Ohio, USA, they still played together almost daily.

They had grown tired of hunting and shooting "marks" on this assassin-themed video game. They both talked about how much they loved the guns and grenades and knives they got to use while killing "marks"—targets for their boss—in order to earn money. He who wins the most money wins the game.

So far, Raj was winning, with a higher body count and more points, and overall money for the methods of kill he performed. Girish, his second cousin on his fathers' side, was close behind in points and money. He preferred to shoot his marks from a distance and that provided less points than killing them up close with a handgun or knife.

Their conversation turned to the normal aspects of life.

"How is the business doing? Is your mom doing better?" Girish typed out on the keyboard.

Raj responded with, "*Amma* seems to be doing okay. Sometimes she just stares off out the window, like she is looking for someone or searching for *abba*, expecting him to come walking into the store, like he would coming back from the bank."

Girish continued to type away. "Are you still selling lots of the 'loosies' you were telling me about?"

Raj smiled. "It's crazy how these *goras*—white people—just roll in and spend *paisa* like it's their *baba's*! Same *gora* will come in three times a week and buy a couple loosies each time! I have some extra green they call 'Benjamins' I am going to send over for you. I got some killer yellow kicks the other day and a new watch with a band that matches the sneaks!"

"That is sooo great of you! I am going to get some new sneaks too!" Girish responds.

Raj types out, "Oh . . . you will be able to get more than a pair of kicks cuz! I will stack you up in *paisa*!"

"Maybe I can save some Benjamins to come see you. My dad's cousins have been talking about coming over to America to look at some buildings next spring. I should ask him to get me a passport so I can come with them."

Girish starts a new game and off they ran to hunt and kill more marks.

In typical Girish fashion, he headed up a flight of stairs with his sniper rifle to find a perch to hide in. He enjoyed laying behind his scope, scanning the crowd of people, looking for his mark.

Raj moved forward into the crowd of people, scanning faces as he went, checking them against his mark's face in the corner of the TV screen. He held a six-inch-long filet knife—handle down in his palm, blade up along his forearm. This time he planned to get close to his mark and maximize his points with some close-in knife work. Too bad the game did not give different points for liver strikes versus heart or lung strikes with a knife. Raj instinctively knew it was far easier to stab a man from behind than look him in the eyes and see the shock as he dies before you.

CHAPTER 18
CLOSE FOLLOW

As I angle across the plaza filled with people, I see the mark, stopping to light a cigarette, head slightly down, looking into the flame. I slow my pace and angle my directional flow to come in behind him.

I had lost him in the crowd of people leaving the courthouse and was breathing a sigh of relief to reconnect. Single-man follows are never easy and normally end in failure—you get burned by the mark or you lose them completely trying not to get burned.

This case should have been over a few months ago with a simple financial settlement from the insurance company. But this dude wanted more ... always more. He just walked out of court after a preliminary hearing for a jury trial on his lawsuit for damages from a car accident over two years ago.

His limp is less pronounced now that no one is there to see his performance. Cigarette lit, he moves off toward a parking lot just down the block from the courthouse. Good thing I had parked in the same lot. I was not able to tail the morning follow into the courthouse, so I needed to rely on the tactic of "most common" used location for him to park at.

At least he was somewhat predictable.

The lot has a large chain link fence around it, gates for entry and exit, as well as a gatehouse—but no guard—with both gates standing straight up. There is no cost to park during court hours.

There is no way we are both going into that open parking lot and him not see me. I pull out my cell phone and act like I am calling someone. My lawyer ... everyone hates their lawyer. "So, what the fuck Marty! What happened in there? You let that bitch wife of mine walk all over us!" I say, loud enough that he is sure to hear, and he does glance over. I use the phone to mask my face as I stalk off toward my vehicle, parked across the lot from the mark's. Hopefully he will just suspect I am another disgruntled man caught in the legal system, being ground to death by dollars, rather than a PI following up on a suspected bogus liability claim.

I give him a beat or two to start out so he is well ahead of me. I have a pretty solid idea of where he is heading, and I want to be there to record it for the insurance company.

I drop a quick text to the Alpha One—aka Face or Boss Man—that Close Follow is rolling. That is all he ever wants—minimal status updates that you are doing the job.

CHAPTER 19

LIBBY

I am heading over to my youngest daughter Libby's house to have lunch with her at a nearby sushi bar. She lives about twenty minutes across the county, and I am traveling through a number of little towns and burgs, which once had some of the oldest steel mills in the state.

Nothing much is left these days but empty factory buildings with broken windows and overgrown fence rows. This was once called the Heart of It All or Steel Valley America. So much steel was produced here during the years of this country's prosperity. That is, until the first big reduction in the workforce in the later 1980s, and then again after the North American Free Trade Agreement—NAFTA—was signed by President Clinton. Jobs continue to leave the area—and the country—to this day. The large corporations that used to, by definition, mean America, like Nabisco, Kraft, GE, Ford, and many others, have been sending work to Mexico and other parts of the world—places without OSHA and the requirement to pay medical benefits and retirement plans.

Then you have companies like Apple, who have over $500 billion of corporate profits in a Bermuda bank made from overseas sales and yet borrow money from banks in the US to fund US operations so they can avoid the income tax on the foreign profits. The cost of borrowing money in the US is less than the corporate tax on the profits, so they call that "good business."

I understand that using the Internal Revenue Service tax code to your best advantage is in fact the very definition of "good business," but at the expense of being a good steward of the people and the country who make you the great company that you are? So many other countries would never permit a profitable concern that was not nationalized. Russia nationalized Gazprom, Japan did so with Tokyo Power, and Britain with Cardiff Airport and Network Rail in 2013.

Today's US corporations do not seem to understand just how good they have it.

My mind is always full of these thoughts as I perform tasks like driving, cleaning the horse and sheep pens, or running cross-country on my farm. The contemplation of the plight of our nation can truly cause me frustration!

As I cross the river and railroad tracks that separate one small town from the next, the audio voice from my Ford F-150 reminds me that the local speed limit is fifteen miles per hour, much less than what I am currently traveling.

I remember my daughter warning me about local lawmen and their strict enforcement of speed limits. I use the brake to slow my truck instead of my normal coasting speed reduction and scan the upcoming parking lots and oncoming cars for signs of light bars and Crown Vics or Explorers, the autos of choice for most law-enforcement agencies.

I make a few dog-leg turns through town until I am on my daughter's dead-end street with just two houses and no edge lines or center line on this three-hundred-foot roadway. I see Libby's white Ford Focus coming toward me. The sunlight is from behind the car so I am able to get a clear view of the driver's compartment. It's not Libby who's driving! A young African American male is behind the wheel of my daughter's car! What the fuck is this all about? She would have told me had she loaned out her car—technically *my* car—which is registered in my name. I also pay the insurance.

The driver also looks surprised. I cut my steering wheel hard to the left, blocking the little street, slamming the gearshift into park, with my left hand knifing under the seatbelt across my body to unclasp the release, as my right hand moves down. I use my left hand to pull my dress shirt up to access the inside-the-waistband, deep-tuck holster with my right. As the distinctive *shnick* of my Smith and Wesson 9mm sounds as the weapon comes clear of the Kydex holster, I rack a round into the pipe and press both hands out into the very stable grip, target focused, watching facial cues for reaction or response, judging threat response.

I know ... *rack a round in the chamber*—it should already be chambered! Look, my dick and I ... we have a relationship—one built on mutual respect and trust. He is just not a fan of having a loaded handgun pointed at him. I somehow feel he has a valid point. After all, it is very unlikely that I will ever need to be in a gunfight, and I can draw and rack with smoothness and efficiency. So, for me, it's a personal choice, like wearing a seatbelt, or sex without a condom. We all make choices.

Scanning the guy in the car, I see no obvious marks on his face. I can't believe he hurt my little girl and got nothing in return! No way that tough little 5'3" beast, who weighs a buck twenty-five and dead lifts 255, wouldn't have delivered a few blows to his face. No red marks, no swelling—nothing but a steady gaze back.

He holds stock still, but not relaxed in his body language. Tense, both hands still on the wheel. This motherfucker has been at gunpoint before. He is thinking, judging, weighing his options.

So, what is the math equation for shooting through the front windshield? Round goes out and rises due to the angle of the glass deflecting it upward, then back through his front windshield. The round should deflect downward. Fuck! *Should* deflect... How much damage to the hollow point after going through *my* windshield? How will the deformity affect reentry through the other windshield? Fuck! I have only practiced shooting out the front windshield at a threat, never back into another vehicle. *FUCK!!!*

When in doubt, center mass. This prick is less than twenty feet away... can't be much trajectory change occurring at this distance. A 9mm round traveling at twelve hundred feet per second will push through four or five layers of drywall and a two by four. These two glass windscreens should be no match for my high-velocity rounds at this distance.

I can't just shoot this fucker who is driving my car—my *daughter's* car. Maybe she loaned it to him. Maybe he is having some type of personal emergency. Where the fuck is my daughter? Is she alright, safe in the house that I can see just beyond the rear of her car?

I need to control this situation, *own* it, so I start with taking my left hand off my weapon and placing it on the truck door handle, pushing it open and pinning it with my left foot, positioning it straight out. Keeping hard eye contact on the target, who is not yet a threat, my ass shifts to the left. My weapon comes off the target, who stays frozen. This is the moment, as you exit the vehicle and re-engage the target, that if he is going to make a move, he does so. This is when time is measured in fractional seconds. If we had been on the range, the shot time would be splitting the seconds into fractions for later analysis and dissection.

As my feet hit the ground and I come around the door jam, his head is swiveling backward to look for his own exit plan. The engine starts to accelerate and the car starts to shift as the gear is changed from drive to reverse.

I come around the engine compartment of my truck in large swinging strides right up to the side window and yell, "Freeze, freeze, freeze!"

His head swivels back around to look at me, one hand on the shifter, the other on the steering wheel, his eyes a little larger now that I am within three feet of his face, weapon held steady, looking through the sights hard at his T-Box—the point where his nose meets his forehead.

I yell through the glass, "Shut it down! Now, you motherfucker!" He pushes the shifter to park and switches the key off, never taking his eyes off of mine.

"Where the fuck is my daughter? Where is Libby?" I say with a crack in my voice, gun held at full extension, two-hand grip pressing tight, elbows starting to strain from being locked out.

"Get the fuck out of the car, asshole! NOW!" Where the fuck is Libby, why does this asshole have her car? I know her boyfriend the meathead body builder is at work an hour away. Has this guy been casing their place? Is she in the trunk being abducted, dead in the house, or bleeding out as I try to get this fucker to respond to my demands? My mind races...Am I sure I can't just shoot him for cause? No. Theft is not part of the "justified use of deadly force." There is no imminent and unavoidable danger of death or grave bodily harm to the innocent. But where the hell is Libby?

In the words of my daughter, "Easy killer...easy." Slow it down, get control, and maintain control. I need to work this out. This is not an area that I have had much training in—Subject Control. Package/Principal Handling, Closer Quarter Protection Details, Combative Pistol, Small Team Movement, yes. But not this, not when it's my kid's life at stake.

Okay...let's try this again. "Open your car door and step out, hands where I can see them. If you run, I will be forced to shoot you! Do you understand?" He nods his head. As his hands work the door lever and the seal of the door breaks, I ask, "Where is Libby?" He remains quiet. Man, if he hurt her in any way...

He continues to exit the car. As he moves to stand up, I move around the back of the vehicle, in the hopes of cutting off a fast run through the few scattered yards. He stands stock still, watching me.

"Walk toward the house! NOW! Move it, asshole!" He walks back toward the house and heads up the short gravel drive toward the front porch. As he gets to the stairs, I look up the three steps to the front door and see that it's ajar.

"Is she in there? Is she all right or am I going to have to fuck you up?"

He speaks for the first time. "I don't know."

I say, "You don't know what?"

He continues up the steps, and pushes the front door to their little two-bedroom, one bath starter home open.

"In," I say. "Get the fuck in the house."

He passes over the threshold, me right behind him. As I clear the door frame I scream, "Libby! Libby! Libby, are you okay?"

I need to check the house, but I can't do so with him in tow. I am not permitted to tie him up or handcuff him or flex cuff or zip tie, or restrain him in any way. That would not be legal for me to do, but sure ... *he* can just take a car and maybe harm my family, but I have to treat him better than he treats society! I can't even lock him in the bathroom. GeeZus this is a fucked-up system. I need to find my daughter and right fucking now!

"On your knees, asshole!" He complies. "Cross your legs at the ankles, lace your fingers tighter and put your hands on top of your head." Just like they do on TV ... Shit. So much of our social training comes from the fucking TV! We need classes on how to perform proper Subject Control, legally, because on TV I am sure the shit they do is not always legal.

As I move around him to start to check the two bedrooms down the short hall, my daughter walks into the kitchen to my right, up from the basement.

She takes in the scene. "Dad! What are you doing? Why do you have my neighbor at gunpoint? What the hell is going on?"

"Your *neighbor?*"

"Yes, that's Justin!"

"What the fuck is he doing driving your car. I mean, MY CAR?"

"What? Justin, do you have my car?" Libby asks.

Justin now decides to be a bit chatty. "I needed it, the door was unlocked, I just needed to meet a guy for a quick minute across the block. I was going to bring it right back."

I remember Libby and meathead Carl talking about their neighbor Justin and what a druggie he is, how he is always bumming money from them or a ride to get smokes. Great ... This little fuck lets himself into my daughter's house and takes her car!

"Hey Justin, how about some time for grand theft auto, dickhead? Really, what the fuck were you even thinking? Seriously, asshole ... spill it!" I say.

He says, "I got to meet my dealer, I am out of pocket, I owe him and he will come hunting me and that would be bad for me and my momma."

I say, "Alright Justin. This is what we are going to do. You are going to walk out the door and run your ass down the block to meet your dealer. You ever come onto my daughter's property again without an express invitation, I will find you and I will eat you for lunch! You got it? Now move! Out with you!"

Justin looks over at Libby. "I can just go?"

She replies with, "Yes, Justin. You can leave."

As he jumps up and turns to leave, I say, "Remember what I said. I will eat you for lunch, you little *fuck*!" He darts out the door and jumps off the landing, running past my truck and down the block toward town.

"Damn it, Libby! What have I told you about locking your doors? This dickhead could have been bad news or his drug dealer may have wanted some young girl as payment. GeeZus! You scared the fuck out of me!" Calming down, I add, softer, "I thought that little asshole had hurt you."

Libby says in her sharp voice that reminds me so much of her mother, "Dad! Calm down. I am fine, the situation is fine. Can you just relax and not want to kill everyone you meet?"

The truth is, I don't want to kill anyone, or even shoot anyone, or even need a gun or a weapon of any kind in my life, but I refuse to be a sheep or a victim, although my family—with the exception of my daughter, Keira, who loves it—resists me trying to teach them what I have learned in the many self-defense tactical firearms training classes I have taken.

"Libby, you know that movie *Taken*, with Liam Neeson? I am not that guy. If someone snatches you, I don't think I have the skills to find you, let alone kill all the bad guys. Just please keep your doors locked," I plead.

Libby says, "Dad, can we just go to lunch?"

I soften my tone, noticing the adrenaline leaving my body. "Let's get your car back into the driveway. We can take my truck for sushi." I feel so heavy and tired ... always tired.

I need to get a coffee on the way to lunch.

CHAPTER 20

SUSHI

"Hey Trevor—swing by that sushi place on the way home," the client asks as we make good time rolling through late-evening traffic, my full team of protective officers and two vehicles just wanting to be done with another long day of hustling a client around the city.

"Yes, sir." I reach over and touch the driver's elbow, at rest on the center console. Once he nods in my direction and I know I have his attention, I say, "We are changing routes of travel. Head toward Miyoto Sushi in front of the mall complex for the client to pick up food." My driver nods again, and continues on.

I key up my mic and radio to the Follow Vehicle the route change and reason, and receive a short "copy" in return from the singleton in the Follow Vehicle who is the driver but also a trained armed security officer. The Tahoe is quiet again as the four of us roll in comfort. Damn, I really love these air-cooled seats on my back. Wearing armor, an undershirt, and a sport coat in the summer really builds up the body heat. All day in and out of the vehicle, moving through buildings and meeting to meeting makes a man enjoy some of the finer comforts of life, even if it is just cold air blowing on his butt crack.

In all, there is myself, the client, the driver for today (Tiger Lily, or John Paul as his mother calls him), and a new guy in this vehicle. Well, new to me. I have never worked with him before. I only run certain jobs. I can't remember his name so I call him "Number Two" all day. The Follow Vehicle's driver is Sean (aka T-1), my long-time mentor and early instructor on firearms. He runs as many of these jobs as he can. He not only loves the work but truly understands the importance of each protective agent's position in the lineup. He ran this stuff with State Department people long ago, and it never left his soul. As a first-rate computer tech for his day job and sneak and peek guy in the past, his massive skill set is invaluable to the job.

We don't get paid for the Follow Vehicle, but I demand it for each job I am on, if for no other reason than my own personal safety. Having another way out from a bad situation or even a flat tire will change the entire day. If ever it is needed, the client is then all too happy to pay for the extra charge of stepping into another ride and continuing with his day without waiting around for a service tow truck or us to get a rental sent out. I just like having more options.

Today's client, Stan Wiley, is a fourth-generation fishmonger from Pittsburgh. His company has helicopters that fly out to tuna and sport fishing boats that are catching tuna to be cut down and sold in his fish market. He supplies fish to everyone from sushi bars within a two-hour drive to soup kitchens who take his scraps.

Bluefin tuna is the prize everyone wants, but all of that ends up in Japan—that network is wildly strong and no one messes with them. Their buyers, or what we call *enforcers*, are owned men who will do anything for The Boss.

Yellowfin tuna is a much smaller fish and more of what is served locally. Not many people could tell the difference by eating it, but the cost is wildly different. It is rumored that Stan has a network of sport fishing captains that will call in a catch and whoever gets a whirly bird to it first gets the prize. This can cause some interesting adventures in a 'copter. Once you get to the boat you have to winch the fish on board and secure it. They weigh up to 300 pounds and this alone can restrict how many men can be on board the bird, and how much fuel it takes to get there and back again.

It is very illegal to have sport fishing turned into a commercial market, but what happens in international waters is an entirely different thing. All the details—like photos, weight, and payment—are all handled via SAT phone or internet connection depending on how far out the boat is. International waters start just twelve nautical miles from shore, and most tuna is well past that mile-marker.

Stan is working his cell phone. I am hoping he is talking to someone he knows at Miyoto who will have his order ready when we roll up. After all, his fish market provides them with their product.

As we roll up to the front of the restaurant, Tiger Lily parks in one of the many empty handicap spots. The Follow Vehicle backs into a spot down the lane, in clear view of us, but standing off so we don't look like we are together.

I key my mic. "I am on the client. The panic call is Swordfish. You know the drill." I exit the vehicle, and, with Stan off my right shoulder, we head toward the entrance.

We have practiced this drill a number of times in our monthly training. On the "panic call" at least a singleton from Vehicle One comes in, takes physical hold of the client, spins him around by grabbing his belt in the back and shoulder, and pushes him forward out the door and into the vehicle, which is now staged for a "strong side" evac. They leave the scene immediately. If I don't come out in thirty seconds, someone from the Follow Vehicle comes in to support me.

The place is crowded. I have been here six times over the past two years and never seen it like this. It is a Friday night, not a normal night for us to stop and much later in the evening as well. The overflowing bar crowd and the waiting-for-a-table crowd have all mixed together in the open area near the hostess stand. She is busily working her tablet and glances up at me. I step aside and let Stan come into view. He smiles broadly, lighting up his face and charming the young Asian hostess. "Carryout order for Wiley Fish Market." She turns and retreats toward the back sushi bar for the pickup order.

My sidestep brushed me into a dude who evidently has been here a long time waiting on a table and burning the edges off his week with what smells like whiskey as he waits. "Sorry, sir," I say, as I make brief eye contact. He glances over at me, taking me in—suit coat, white dress shirt, no tie, badge of my security company on my belt. I am scanning the crowd, checking the bar area, watching for threats.

"Fucking cops just pushing little people around!" the drunk dude says.

"Sorry man … just making room for other people coming in," I say, with a smile that is anything but friendly. I need to move this guy off.

"You cops just think you own the place, always telling us what to do! Stand over here, walk this line." Obviously, I am dealing with someone who has had more than one field sobriety test and failed. He turns and squares up to me. Shit! I would not have expected this happening at a sushi bar.

I key my mic. "Swordfish, Swordfish, Swordfish!" I turn toward Drunk Guy. "You don't want to do this, especially here." I put both hands up, palms out in a nonthreatening way, oftentimes referred to as the "interview stance" by law enforcement. It looks harmless and unprovoked, but gets your hands up in the work space in case defensive action is needed. My peripheral vision catches the main door being yanked open as Number Two comes in. Stan is unceremoniously snatched up, spun around, and bodily pushed toward the doorway, which has not even finished closing.

Now that my client is safely out of harm's way, I smile a wolf's smile at Drunk Guy.

T-1, hearing the panic call of "Swordfish," pops his vehicle door and turns his watch face up, watching the second hand. After Stan is shoved into the back seat with the agent over top of him, Vehicle One is away. At the 20-second mark, T-1 is moving toward the entry door, a little worried and a little excited.

As he yanks the door open, I am just stepping out, carryout order in my left hand. His eyes fly open. "Dude, what happened?"

I respond, "Nothing my one little finger could not handle."

He falls in beside me as we head to the Follow Vehicle. I key up the mic. "Safe and clear. Repeat—all safe and clear, meet at rally point." In this case, one mile from our location, same side of the road as our original travel direction.

Keeps it simple.

CHAPTER 21

THE SAME CRAZY DREAM

The smartphone alarm is sounding. Amazon rainforest birds are squawking. At each passing moment it gets louder and louder. I jerk awake to the 5 am alarm, turning it off, and drop my head back on the pillow.

My wife, Sofia, drapes her leg across mine, locking me in place beside her in bed. This is her cue that I need to sleep in and not get up to work out. My regimented routine is being broken today. Sometimes we don't sleep at all because she has ... other plans.

She purrs into my ear, "How did you sleep, honey?"

I respond, "I had that strange dream again. The one where I am in some European country with my team."

"Tell me the entire dream again. Maybe I can find something new or link a meaning to why you keep having it," she says. She lays her head on my shoulder, her hand over my heart.

"Like last time ... we are a four-man team rolling in an SUV in a foreign country. None of us speak the language. I am the oldest by many years and the number four guy. I only know one other team member, T-1.

"The vehicle stops a block away from the location and I roll out to go to a quickie market for 'make due' medical supplies—tape, towels, alcohol ... You try not to look like you are buying medical supplies. As I walk toward the location, I can smell the heat and dust in the air. Not like in Greece where all you smell is diesel engine smog, but fine dirt particles.

"It's a small, family-owned place and a teenage son is following me around the store, trying to help me pick stuff. I can feel the dirt and gravel under my boots crunch as we move about. He speaks a little English, but not much. We get to the register. I was able to get all of the needed supplies.

"A large explosion many blocks off rattles the glass in the windows as I finish paying for the supplies. The shock wave passes through, kicking up dust all around. I wave off the change and head for the door. Car alarm horns begin to honk from the explosion's shock wave. A large plume of thick, black smoke reaches toward the sky.

"The team vehicle rolls up to the front door. T-1 meets me on the steps as I come out, and we jump into the SUV and it rolls out, the driver doing a great job moving through the mixture of vehicle and pedestrian traffic."

Sofia starts to ask the questions that I will not have the answers for. "Did your team cause the explosion or is your team trying to stop it? Are the medical supplies directly for you four or for a larger team you are part of, staged nearby? Could the medical supplies be for your next overt action or simply precautionary.? Why doesn't the team have medical blowout kits for each man? Were you armed? Handguns or rifles?"

"I do remember being armed, a handgun at my four o'clock position, under my lightweight green jacket. I also had on soft armor, in a compression shirt, close to my body. If we would have had rifles, I am sure I would have had plates on instead of soft armor.

"The explosion did not seem to be a surprise to me, but I also remember in the dream thinking, 'Fuck, that is bad.'"

"Dreams are strange," Sofia says. "They are the subconscious mind trying to deal with life. You are working on the strange case for FinCEN ... That is unchartered water for you. This dream could just be your mind trying to deal with so many unknowns. The team is a common archetype for you. Having people you know, like Sean—T-1—there for support, working together. The gun is nothing more than a comfort for your ability to not feel completely alone or lost and helpless." She continues with, "What do you always say? The mind is the weapon, the gun or knife is just the tool?"

I am surprised she repeats that statement, even though I say it often. Rare is the day a man feels his wife hears him be prophetic.

We lay in the dark, talking about so many things—her job, and how crazy her patients are, my jobs, the kids, the hobby farm, the law-enforcement training. Before you know it, the 6 am alarm goes off. No Amazon rainforest birds this time. Just the loud, classic alarm clock sound. I sit up, swinging my feet to the floor. Feeling the pain in my joints, bones, and muscles, the old man groan slips past my lips as I stand to get dressed and feed the farm.

CHAPTER 22
SEVEN-DOLLAR FELONY

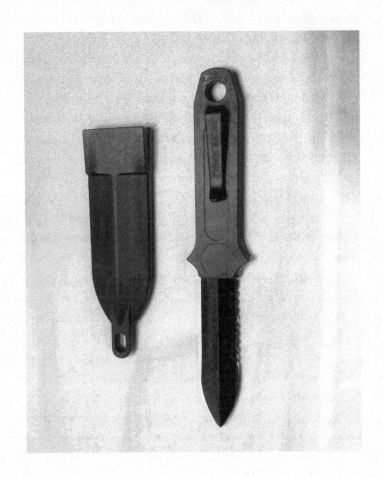

I gave Limper, as I call him, a lot of room, figuring he would park in the same lot for court again today. I caught a space a half block closer at a meter. As I stuffed quarters into the slot, I glanced toward the lot to see him getting out of his car.

I moved off toward the courthouse, wanting to get in before he made me, assuming he got a look at me last time I was doing *close follow*.

I left my Go Bag in the vehicle—handgun, holsters, spare mags, smoke, OC spray, and other essential tools of the trade, depending on what the day called for. Today it was a sport coat, white shirt, blazer, and black dress shoes. The only contraband I had was a hardened plastic punch knife in a plastic sheath, on a clip tucked into my pants.

Not sure why I felt the need to keep it on me. Normally I carry a large spring folder clipped to my inside pocket, but courts frown on those. This was a stealth alternative that really was not necessary. There was no known threat, but it was difficult to walk around naked. Well, not completely naked. I do take Brazilian jiu-jitsu. Always a White Belt, as they say—always learning.

As my wife Sofia recently quoted back to me, *The mind is your weapon, all else are just tools.* But it does provide a sense of comfort to have a tool on you, even if it is hardened plastic.

This courthouse uses old-school metal detectors manned by local sheriff deputies, some of whom I know personally and others whom I have trained with and know by reputation. I was not overly concerned with anyone finding my $7.00 knife, but it is always uncomfortable to me to break the rules. Well, more than just rules. I think this would be referred to as a felony, a *seven-dollar felony* at that. Could I be more ignorant? The fact is, I have a number of these hard plastic knives. I pick them up at gun shows. This one in particular I liked because of the hilt clip that holds it in place on the inside of your pants. Alpha One—aka Face—and I were walking around looking over the gear and guns at a show when I found it.

This was as much a test about me as anything. My motto had always been "No Felonies!" and the guys I roll with are more like, "Don't get *caught* doing felonies." Necessity would be the deciding factor, but how do you become comfortable with breaking the law, unless you break the law?

Dropping my keys and phone into the bowl, I walked through the metal detector. It beeped and my stomach dropped. I tasted acid in my mouth and I was sure my pupils were dilating. I turned around and a small line was forming at the door. Great ... more stress. I walked back around and the guard suggested I take off my watch. I added it to the bowl and walked through again. No sounds made. I retrieved my items from the bowl and headed off to the courtroom. The spike in adrenaline was noticeable. That was some wild shit.

The knife was still firmly in place as I walked up the stairs to the courtroom.

CHAPTER 23

RAJ AND THE DRUG DEALER, PART FIVE

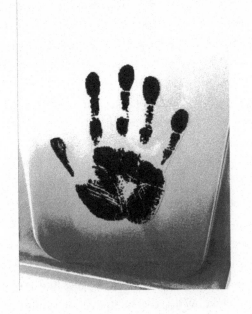

Raj's phone lights up with a text message from Chance: "Yeah I can meet. Where at?"

It is Sunday and the Q-Mart closes at 6 pm, which is earlier than usual. Raj will help his mother close and get home. They will make supper together and then he can go out to meet with Chance.

He texts back: "The pizza place across from the high school at 8." The reply is a thumbs-up emoji.

At exactly 8 pm, Raj watches Chance roll into the parking lot in his old Camaro, freshly painted canary yellow, just a shade different than Raj's shoes and the band on his Shinola watch.

Raj is smiling from ear to ear. "Love the new color of your Camaro, man!"

"Thanks. And no, I did *not* use your shoes as inspiration. This is an original factory color for my Camaro." Tossing a cigarette butt to the ground from his open window, Chance says, "So, what's up. What do you need? More product? I have some buried in the back."

Raj shakes his head. "What if I don't want to do this anymore?"

"Do what?"

"Sell loosies anymore."

Chance shrugs. "Dude. That is up to you. But I think you got a great thing going. You are moving product, you get no heat from anyone I hear of, you are being honest with your customers ... Some of them have moved up to me and are buying in larger quantities than you're selling. Honestly, man ... I don't see an issue. You got to be stacking fat cash."

"Well, that's just it. The bank doesn't want any more of it," Raj says.

Chance's eyes widen. "Dude! What the fuck did you say? You are taking cash to the bank? What the fuck are you thinking? You *stack* cash, bro ... meaning you *hide* it. Buy shit with it, stick it in a shoebox in your closet, but don't ever take it to the bank! You will send up the smoke to the feds and they will be down here in a minute, fucking up this entire gravy train of ours *big time*! Dude ... if you hear anything—I mean anything *at all*—about someone snooping around, you have got to tell me so we can shut this thing down and bail. If Jean-Pierre finds out you got heat on you, it *will* go badly, bro! I mean *really* badly! That dude and his people don't fuck around. If he thinks you set him up or burned him, he will kill everyone and everything you know!" Taking a drag on a fresh cigarette and lowering his voice, Chances adds, "I saw it once in Detroit. I was working on bringing a good-sized load down and Jean-Pierre took me to this large abandoned office building. We walked up a fuck-ton of steps and inside this one room they got this dude tied to a big support post. Dude is naked and covered in old dried blood and new, *seeping* blood. Looked like they had been at this dude for fucking *hours*. It was fucking cold in that place. This dude is shivering so hard his teeth are banging together. Jean-Pierre just rolls into the room, looks the guy over, dude is sobbing, recognizes my man and starts this incoherent babble, begging for his life. Fuck dude ... it was terrifying to even be in that room."

Raj's eyes grow wide as his fear becomes palpable. There's an acid taste in his mouth as he reaches for his cherry pop to try and wash it down. There's no longer a sweetness in his drink ... the bubbles bring no happiness to his taste buds and the acid taste is worse.

"Chance ... what have I gotten myself into?" Raj says without thinking.

Chance replies, "Nothing to worry about, bro ... unless you find someone snooping. And if you do, you'd better take care of that shit and *quick*."

"How do I do that?"

"Damn, son ... You just call your boy Chance. I will take care of any problems you have. I got a squad of warriors who can get shit done in a flash. You see something funny, you just call me."

Raj takes another slug of his pop, feeling a little better. Chance will help him if something comes up.

This time, the pop tastes fine—sweet and bubbly and good—and he relaxes a little more.

CHAPTER 24

SINGLE-DIGIT COLD

It is cold ... single-digit cold. I lay prone, pressed against the earth. I can feel the warmth of my body seep out of me and into the frigid earth below me.

The moisture created by my warm body is melting the snow beneath me, passing through my pants and long underwear, as the wind pushes snow across my field of view. My Leopold Scope is clear, but visibility is poor. These are not promising long-distance shooting conditions!

The ceramic plates in my kit help to keep my core warm and suspend me off the ground a few extra inches. I adjust the bi-pod legs to account for the angle and the distance of my anticipated shot. There will be no room for error or time for a second shot. My breathing is a little labored from the pressure of the plates on my diaphragm. The only sound is the wind rattling the snow along the ground, which sounds a lot like the shifting sand of another land. A small snow drift is forming around my body and the along the rifle.

Damn I'm cold ... Within twenty minutes I will be too cold to effectively make my shot. My muscles will start to tighten up, my hands will fail in the commands that the mind will send to them, basic motor skills will not only diminish but fail all together. This shit needs to happen ... soon!

Overwatch or blocker, gun of last resort, is just that—the guy who never gets to shoot, but is required to never miss a shot.

The others are much closer to the target location. Waiting as I am, when the scream comes, it shocks me to the core. My blood freezes inside my veins and a shiver runs its icy finger up my spine.

The scream lasts far longer than I expected, a full fifteen seconds, an eternity if it is you under that knife ... And then ... *silence*. Deafening silence. The snow swirls around my confused eyes and interrupts my brain pattern. I am momentarily lost in old thoughts of long ago.

A single shot, muffled by the wind and the distance, reaches my ears and mind. I come back to the present, press into the stock, load up on the bi-pod, and watch for a squirter.

Sure enough, one lurches into my peripheral field of view. I can tell by the diminutive frame it's a female. *Well shit!* I think. At that moment, the scream comes again, piercing through the cold, thin air. My heart skips a beat, and I jerk a little, unnerved by the sights and sounds in front of me.

I slip my finger into the trigger well. I find her in the crosshairs of the scope. Mentally I calculate distance to confirm my MOA—minute of angle—hold point, distance of travel, angle of movement and range to target—all while taking up slack in the trigger.

The female slows, looking back over her shoulder in the direction of the heavy shot. Talking to my right index finger, I whisper, "Press, press, press ..." The break is clean. I am visually out in front of my target. The report pushes the weapon and scope off center, and when I am able to see clearly again, the field of view is completely empty, as though nothing has ever been there. She has just been a dream ... floating across the open space.

Yet the panicked screams are still stuck in my head.

Was I too far out in front for the 2,500 feet per second round to find its mark? Picking my face from the locked position on the stock, I scan the area. Nothing. She must be done. Nowhere for her to go but down. But nothing to confirm I made a kill shot ... no tell at all. The shot felt good, it felt right. A little unnerving, but it seemed clean.

I break free of the frozen earth, my legs stiff from the cold, not wanting to respond to the commands of the brain. I push my weapon out in front of me at high ready and moved forward. I cover the 350 yards in moments. I can see her lying there, clearly dead, no movement, the wind mussing her hair, empty, no-thing, nothing more.

I always feel that confusion of pride in a job done cleanly and melancholy for the end of life. The shock of that 7.65 × 54 round stops everything, simply shuts down the central nervous system completely—no involuntary muscle twitch, no gurgle of air and blood in the lungs, nothing but instant death and quiet ... the stone-cold silence of death.

I reach down, grabbing the bitch coyote by the back leg and sling her over my shoulder, proud of the blood that I'll have on my winter white camo. The guys come out of the timber carrying her partner in crime, a very large male.

Two shots, two dead sheep killers, the home range and farm safe again from predators. That squealing rabbit in distress call really works, even if it does turn your blood cold!

Sitting around the old milk room of the hundred-plus-year-old barn, there is nothing like the smell of fresh coffee brewing, and the gentle sound of sheep baaing out in the main barn.

The coyotes are laid out on the concrete, fresh blood pooling at the edge of the floor drain. I am finally warm again. The old ceramic John Deere thermostat on the wall reads 52 degrees. Compared to the single digits we just endured, this is a heat wave.

The guys are stripping off the outer layers of winter camo, reliving the morning predawn hunt. There are English deer skull mounts on the wall, bleached white, deer antlers hanging from a peg on the wall, an old deer hide hanging over the back of a chair, and a pile of old leg-hold traps in the corner waiting till next fall to be set again in the creeks and edges of the fields.

CHAPTER 25

ACCOUNT REVIEW WITH
DEEPTI NIMBALKAR

As I park my Tahoe in the side lot of the Q-Mart, I am thinking about the last time I saw Deepti Nimbalkar. It was about ten days after her husband's funeral. We met at my office that day to sign all the documents needed to transfer his retirement funds into her name as beneficiary and remove his name from the joint investment account. We updated her beneficiary forms to her son Rajesh, their only child.

She was so sad that day, so quiet and somber, that I was surprised that her brother was not with her. He is oftentimes at the Q-Mart when I stop in to see them or pick up some convenience item on my way home from work. He would be covering the store counter, and Rajesh would be working the beverage tunnel.

Rajesh and his uncle seemed to get along. I had heard them talk about how Rajesh and one of the cousins from India play video games together. With an eleven-hour time difference, the logistics had to be challenging, but kids today never seem to need sleep. Me ... I always want a nap!

The family is set up for six-month investment reviews, but I had let a few extra months slip by. First, I'm not really good at how to talk to people after a loved one dies, and second, I feel guilty as fuck being here now that FinCEN has pinned me down and forced me to help find out the connection with some relative in India who has some kind of ties to a radical Muslim faction. I always thought Indians were Hindu, but I guess about ten percent of the continent's population is Muslim ... That's 195 million people! Holy hell, that's a lot— more than half the entire US population! The US only has about one percent of the population, or about 3.4 million Muslims, living here. And I have read that a sizable number of the Muslim population are Shia, with that sect being broken up into the Twelvers and Ismailis—names I have never heard of but read about recently in my study to try to help our government catch some bad guys.

I am truly not sure how these other religions work. I remember being Presbyterian and wanting to marry a Catholic girl and the uproar that created, and we all believed in the same things and in the same God, so I can't image how having totally different beliefs would affect all of that. I do know history, and people have been killing each other over religious beliefs for centuries. Probably millennia.

So often I think that I am worldly until I read about country populations, or very old civilizations! Just wild the number of people in countries all over the world. How you're supposed to find a single bad guy or a group of people with bad intent must be a crazy challenge for the NSA and other federal agencies.

Deepti greets me from behind the counter as I come through the door, with her soft, singsong voice that brings instant comfort to my soul. My guilt level increases tenfold as I think about how I am to find out who FinCEN is looking into that is somehow related to her.

She finishes up with a customer buying a bag of powdered-sugar donuts, an energy drink, and paying for five dollars in fuel—a rail-thin, long-haired dude with ink all over his arms. To me, he screams junkie. Is it wrong to think that thought? To be biased or to stereotype, as they call profiling in some circles, which is a term that sounds better—at least to me.

Deepti's brother moves into my peripheral vision, coming from the drive-through tunnel into the store. He nods his head to me and mumbles a greeting. He steps in around Deepti and tells her to take me to the office for our meeting. He will handle the front.

The office is small. Nothing has changed since I was here to meet with her husband. It is crammed full of merchandise that does not fit in the stock area. Nothing is fancy or high end. It's all very utilitarian in nature and all function with no form. I can smell spices or incense that was recently burned, which is always an exotic odor to me.

I am a good talker and I go on about how great it is that her brother can help so much and that Raj is able to handle the beverage tunnel. She talks about how well Raj's sales have been going. He's had a significant increase—not large sales but lots of small sales with high margins on those products.

I think it still must be difficult to earn a living on the profits of a five-dollar item. You would really need to sell a bunch of them. But places like dollar store chains seem to be popping up all over place the past few years. Just another niche market to be filled, and obviously the math somehow works.

"Do you have any family in India that came for Jalaj's funeral?" I ask, hoping to lead the conversation.

"Oh yes, Jalaj's brother Devendra came. He is the only other one in the family who has a passport. He travels a lot so it was simple for him to get here. My *amma*, Raj's grandmother, really wanted to come, but she is so old and travel is very hard. Normally we send one of the family over to escort her back."

I ask, "Has Raj ever gotten to go to your home?"

Deepti smiles. "Yes. Five years ago, for the funeral of his *nānī*—his paternal grandmother. He got to see his cousins and has kept in contact with them. Some of them have very different religious beliefs than we do. My family are all Hindu, but part of his family are Muslim and Shia!"

I ask, "How does that even happen?"

"I would think much like someone in this country becoming a Mormon or raised in one religion and becoming Agnostic," Deepti says. I nod my head, trying to think of a way to keep this thread of discussion going. My pause must be too long, because she asks, "How are the investment accounts doing during these strange political times?"

Once we are nearly done reviewing the financial aspects of the recent investment changes that I have made to their models, I decide to try one more question. Not a question from the "playbook" I was given, but something more gentle.

"Will Raj be going over to bring your mother back this year?"

"Yes, yes!" she says. "And his cousin Girish and his father are planning to come along."

"Will they stay with you? Do you have room for all of them?"

"Oh no. They will stay with other family around town. I do not have the room or the temperament for their religious views, and I am too old to be taking orders from a man that is not my husband!" she says with a wink and a smile. I note this independent streak and file it away.

Well, as little as I managed to get, this will still make a solid report to good old Philip Daniels at FinCEN.

As I finish up the review of her account's performance, she thanks me strongly for the continued help and support since Jalaj passed. I sheepishly smile and tell her that it is truly an honor to help her family and to have known them for so very long. A pang of guilt creeps in through the cracks in my suit of armor.

As I am leaving, I can't help but notice the line of cars waiting for the drive-through tunnel. Raj is really making it happen. It always amazes me that this little town has three convenience stores, all within sight of each other, and there are always cars at all of them!

CHAPTER 26
BROKEN WINDOWS

The security industry is very large, broad, and deep, meaning different security companies provide an incredibly wide range of services, with very few trying to handle it all.

Because of this, many security firms work well with each other to accommodate the client. We all want a happy client, which brings us more work, so, if one security company is lacking in static guards for a company employee entrance or factory goods loading area, guys from different companies will come together to get the job done. Of course, everyone wants to get paid.

In our state, each company that you work for is required to provide you with a "White Card" or security guard card. It comes from the state, and on the back is outlined your level of security duties you may perform.

If you work unarmed, it will note that. If you work armed, it will note what weapons you are qualified on through certification to use as tools— revolver, semiautomatic handgun, and shotgun. The state does not have qualifications for armed security with the AR-15, or other less-lethal ammunition, like rubber rounds for the shotgun, bean bag rounds, and so on.

All of the firms that I have worked with require their own training regiment on top of the state-mandated training. You will get additional certification with OC spray and capsaicin spray—referred to as pepper spray. Certainly not the most exciting training you would do. But possibly the most effective tool for crowd control. The spray irritates the membranes in your eyes, nose, and mouth and causes swelling and mucus. Then there's the temporary blindness, difficulty breathing, skin irritations, and a burning sensation that feels pretty much like your skin is melting off your face.

Temporary blindness gives security personnel or law-enforcement officers time to gain control of the subject. And because you have created a situation of blindness and difficulty breathing, it is your personal responsibility to care for that individual. In other words, if they get hurt because you sprayed them and they stumbled into traffic, that is a direct result of your actions and is *your* liability.

Each tool a security officer or law-enforcement officer carries requires training and certification from the state or the company for which you work. You may only use those tools in a manner consistent with the training that you have received.

Security guards oftentimes carry handcuffs, even though they do not have arresting authority. They may detain an individual and put restraints on them for their own safety or the safety of the officer or others as a means of controlling the subject.

Other training you would be expected to receive, depending on what your company specializes in, could be Stops and Approaches of vehicles on your client's property with unknown persons driving around. There's also Building Search, Personal Protection of Principal, Executives Protection, Defensive Driving, and many more.

The company for whom I work, Atlas International Security Corporation, works closely with a local company that provides monitored alarm services for home and business. They had come to us some years back so the owners of the alarm company could get firearms training for themselves and a few of the key employees that are out in the public. This was more from a Conceal and Carry standpoint than a protection of property or people.

That relationship has led to crossover work. We regularly refer our clients to them for the monitored alarm and camera service and they oftentimes utilize Atlas for clients who want someone to watch their home while they are at a funeral of a family member, or on vacation.

Some of those are simply a marked security vehicle with an officer in the driveway for a few hours, to daily stops and outside home perimeter searches and, if something is amiss, they can call for a key holder to enter the property if required. Some clients even prefer security guards to stay on the premises when they are away who work in rotating shifts. Each plan is built off what the specific client is looking for.

One area we enjoy is Executive Protection. Sounds exciting, I know, and it does cause one to be a little more on their "A-Game" due to the seriousness and nature of the work. However, we have had a number of clients employ the Executive Protection guards more as chauffeurs for airport dropoffs, big city meetings when parking is impossible, or even shopping trips. I've shared some of my experiences in this area. No valid threat, but a client who desires that higher level of protection when out and about and the best-quality service available can do no better than Atlas, which is always ready to serve.

Face, Atlas's owner, gets a call from our contact at the alarm monitoring company that they referred one of their largest clients to us for some investigative work at their facility.

The client—let's call them "Get Well, Inc."—has a number of buildings in the downtown area of a sizable city a few counties west of us. They employee a few thousand people and have a security company that manages employee flow at entrances and employee termination with the HR Department, but that is about the extent of their duties and expertise.

Get Well, Inc. is having a problem with broken windows. Well, not *completely* broken out, but spiderwebbed, which still require replacement. This has been going on for about a year, and they have tried many methods to find out who is causing the damage. To date they are over $200,000 in costs for glass breakage. This is affecting the company insurance policy and generally pissing off the owners.

Get Well, Inc. had contacted the alarm monitoring company to see about installing glass breakage window pucks or glass breakage sound sensors in the building to alert the static security guards to the issue so they could better detect a vehicle on one of their many cameras or catch a person driving away.

The added cost of these window pucks and sound sensors was going to be significant, so our contact at the company suggested an alternative idea of having a security company come in as an investigative service to get to the bottom of the mystery.

In order to be cost-effective and make the monitoring company proud, they suggested Atlas. The client had been happy with our work and agreed.

The first step was to analyze the video footage and known damage information quickly and put a plan in place to catch whoever was doing this.

Face put together a three-man team consisting of myself, T-1, and Tiger Lily.

T-1 is a computer geek like few others, and has the shooting skills of an operator. His sketchy pasts leads one to think he was somehow attached to Homeland Security or some nefarious type of work he just never got caught doing, but the dude is good at his craft.

T-1 scanned the video footage around the times that windows were reported cracked. Of all the windows broken, only one was actually heard by an employee as it broke, and he didn't *see* the window break—he just heard the noise. He didn't even report it until he saw maintenance replacing the window a few days later and it dawned on him what had occurred.

The major challege is that Get Well, Inc. has so many buildings on its campus, with city streets running between all of them, that pedestrian and vehicle traffic is constant.

T-1 was able to pull some footage of a few vehicles acting strangely—slow speeds, slight swerves. But nothing linking to the times of known action. Another challenge we found is that the cameras are set high on the buildings, so you can't see plate numbers.

It is our collective assumption that, based on the evidence we do have (and don't have), that it is a pellet rifle. Pellet guns are very quiet, the lead round traveling at 700 to 900 feet per second, and many of the window are fifty feet up, making us think a pistol would not be as accurate or effective. A pellet gun's sweet spot of accuracy occurs at about one hundred feet.

The tensile strength of tempered safety glass is typically four to five times greater than that of quarter-inch glass—oftentimes referred to as "single-strength" glass. Strangely enough, glass is considered a liquid due to its molecular structure even though it is "solid" at normal temperatures. Because of this, glass is prone to defects and impurities that can cause it to perform differently than anticipated.

A quarter-inch object, weighing 77 grains, well under a quarter of an once, traveling at 60 feet per second or approximately 40 miles per hour, will typically shatter tempered glass.

We are also confident that it is two people working together—a driver and a shooter. The shooter can be lying down in the back seat and not even need to stick the barrel out the window. He can just lower the window half way and make the shot as they travel slowly down the roadway.

Many of the lower floors are executive offices and those windows do have glass breakage monitors on them, and it is our further assumption that this is a former employee who feels wrongly terminated and knows a fair amount about the company and the building setup.

My personal thinking is it's someone older, mature in their thinking, a real planner. He does not want to get caught, and so far, he has a fool-proof plan to not get noticed. He, and yes, I am sure it is a male, has been breaking windows for a year. If it was juveniles or young people, they tend to want to be noticed, to get responses, and they oftentimes will escalate the damage or add "tags" to the building to take gang-type credit for their actions.

Not this guy. He takes his time and continues with his assault with enough consistency to affect the company's bottom line profitability with nothing but broken glass.

We have already compiled a potential list given to us by their HR that goes back over five years. Being that my initial thought is maintenance/janitorial, or perhaps a male nurse, I review terminations in those areas first.

We have even considered the husband of a female patient who died in the care of the facility. If he feels that the facility is at direct fault for her death, this could be his method of getting even with Big Corporate America Greed.

The majority of the windows seem to be broken midweek, Wednesday or Thursday, and late at night—after 11 pm and before 6 am. Makes sense. There are less people working those floors. Or perhaps this is an individual or individuals, including the driver, who work a shift that gives them Wednesday and Thursday off, and considering the times of the broken windows, perhaps they work the afternoon turn and perform this vandalism after their work shift or after they have stopped off for a few shots of liquid encouragement.

After pooling and analyzing our data, T-1, Tiger Lily, and I spend thirty minutes building out an action plan to provide coverage on the known days and times, hoping to catch a break in the case so we can apprehend this vandal. We check with some of the other sizable businesses in the general area to see if they have experienced a similar glass breakage issue and although they do have broken windows, none fit our consistent situation, adding credence to our hypothesis that it is someone connected to Get Well, Inc.

CHAPTER 27

ANOTHER ENCOUNTER WITH
MR. PHILIP DANIELS

I am reviewing Martin "Marty" Kohen's retirement plan with him, discussing the finer points of his investment holdings and key economic data and how we feel it will impact the next quarter and his model of investments. My cell phone, sitting on the corner of my conference table—which is made of old oak barn beams—lights up and vibrates, audible enough that Marty and I both look over at the caller ID, which reads: Blocked Caller.

I pick up the phone as I stand, and tell Marty, "I need to take this. I'll be back shortly."

I cross the hall and walk into the kitchen area, closing the maplewood door with clear glass panels behind me. I am fairly sure who the caller is. I have only seen Blocked Caller one other time, and chose not to answer it. The three follow-up calls encouraged me to do so, like I am doing now.

"This is Trevor," I answer.

"Philips Daniels here. How are you this day?" The head of FinCEN Cleveland is being his normal formal self and far more friendly than usual, which immediately puts me on edge.

"I am good, Mr. Daniels," I say, cutting through the clutter of niceness. "What can I help you with today?"

"Give me an update!"

"I turned in my email update last night. Did you not receive it?"

"I received it. It says nothing of interest. No actions taken. Little activity, if any ... What are you actually doing to achieve the goals here?"

Willing myself not to lose it with this dick, I say, through clenched teeth, "I don't understand. I met with Deepti Nimbalkar as you requested. I asked her all the leading questions your office provided. I shared all of that with you weeks ago ... What came out of those details?"

His tone of voice gets harder. "*Nothing.* That information is just not good enough!"

Damn, I think, *this dude would be a prick to be married to. Fuck him!*

Out loud I say, "Look. I am helping as much as I know how. If I'm not meeting your goals, then give me something to move forward on!"

A second of silence and then, "We have the Currency Transaction Report filed by the bank that started this process. We also have the envelope of cash Rajesh mailed to his cousin Girish over in that little town south of Mumbai.

Girish's family are Muslim. Surprisingly, Deepti's are Hindu. But some of Girish's people are clearly radical from what I am getting out of NSA."

"This isn't the first time you've mentioned radical Muslims, Mr. Philips. How is this something I should be involved in? This is no longer a money laundering racket ... Sounds to me like you're chasing terrorists."

Taking a deep breath, like a teacher dealing with a student who just doesn't get the lesson, Mr. Prick launches into a speech: "Money oftentimes leads back to organized crime, and organized crime derives income from many sources—drugs, women, information. To many people, what we call organized crime is just a form of business. Who makes it legal or illegal is purely arbitrary to them. They need to make money to survive, and therefore they do, by any means possible. The threads run deep all around the world. There is always someone else to contend with, someone always willing to fill the void. Rare is the day when we find a threat so loose as this one and that drive-through convenience store. We are trying to figure out if the entire store and family are just a front or if the family is masterminding the entire operation."

When I am sure his speech is finished, I say with authority, "I have known these people for years. Never once have I heard any conversation that would lead me to think they were not good, solid citizens of this country!"

"I don't really care what you think. You are not paid to find weakness and larceny ... That is *my* job! You need to go back in there and put some pressure on them with that line of questions we provided you. And don't send me any more of those useless emails with no progress!" The line goes dead without another word spoken. The fucking arrogant prick! I *wish* I was being paid by these bastards! I need to speak with Dave Honeycut, head of Compliance at my broker/dealer again. I am just not comfortable burning down a client and a relationship like this. There is simply no way my clients are money launderers, let alone terrorists.

I walk back in and sit down to continue with Marty, who says, "That did not go well. You look incredibly stressed and I could hear your raised voice all the way in here."

Shit. I should have been more careful. "Sorry Marty, but my job can get strange at times. I answer to so many people of authority and all of them want to cover their butts. This is one of those cases." In reality it was not one of "those cases." I have never seen anything like this in my entire thirty-plus-year career. The stress of it is getting to me.

How the hell am I supposed to go back into that Q-Mart and find out what Philip Daniels wants?

CHAPTER 28
OFFICE WARNING

The sun was shining brightly through the office window, right into my assistant Noel's eyes. She tucked her head down a little so it was below the counter to shade her from the late-afternoon sun. In Northeast Ohio you never hide from the sunshine. We get so little of it, you simply find a way to protect your eyes from it, and let its warmth seep in.

The front door of the office opened and the chime sounded on the alarm panel. The door swung shut on its automatic closer with a heavy *thunk*. Noel was in the middle of working on a spreadsheet, so she took a moment to hit save before she looked up, fully expecting to see an express delivery driver, about the only nonclient visitors we ever get.

Instead of the typical uniform and polite smile she expected to see, Noel found herself looking into the heavily dilated pupils of a drug addict! Scroungy clothes, nervous pacing, twitchy attitude—the works!

Tweaker man said, "Is the boss here?"

"No he isn't," Noel manages to reply, surprised this guy is standing here. The office is in a really nice area of the community, off the main road, with very limited foot traffic, other than clients with scheduled meetings.

"I need to give him a message ... a *lesson*," he continues, almost shouting.

"*Sir*, you need an appointment. Plus, he's just not here!" Noel states.

Tweaker man quickly steps up against the counter, causing Noel to reach down and lay her hands on an extra-large canister of Mace. The safety was always kept off. All she had to do was press the large red button and point in the general direction of threat and *boom*—instant day of suck for whomever is on the other end of the resulting burning face and eye pain! The thought occurred to her to simply hit the panic alarm switch and alert the alarm company. Of course, they would take the time to call the office before they dispatched police, which would take a few minutes. Then they would need to contact the police and *that* would take a few minutes. *Then* the police station, although close, is still a few more minutes away.

All those minutes could be very bad with a determined intruder.

Lifting the canister up above the counter and pointing it at the tweaker, she shouted, "Get the fuck out! *Now!*"

Seemingly unfazed by her words or the canister of Mace, Tweaker man cocked his head and said, "You want to play it that way?" before turning and walking out the door.

Noel set down the Mace and ran over to the front door, throwing the deadbolt before running into the office that faces the parking lot and looking out to see what car the tweaker was driving. No front plate! *Fuck!* The state of Ohio just did away with that requirement in the past year or so.

Tweaker man was walking away from his car and through the parking lot. Shit! My SUV was in the lot. She figured I must have arrived as she was threatening to Mace the creep! All of a sudden, tweaker man bolted forward, out of Noel's line of sight. Seconds later she heard loud yelling, and she headed for the door.

CHAPTER 29

ENCOUNTER WITH TWEAKER MAN

As I turn off the four-lane onto a quiet residential side street, I can see my office three hundred yards down on the left—the long, curved driveway passing through the well-manicured lawn and shrubs, the craftsman-style building fitting perfectly with the surrounding neighborhood of very high-end homes. The few commercial lots are well appointed and low profile and off the beaten path of travel. In fact, the road is a very long dead-end street.

An older model, dark colored, dirty SUV is parked in the "visitor" parking space nearest the front door. I coast past on my way to the rear of the building, and reverse into my space. I don't have a meeting in my appointment book for this time of day, but clients stop by often enough to drop off investment-related information that they want me to review that it's not a complete surprise to have a visitor.

Any time a vehicle is in my lot or rolls by the building slowly it piques my interest. My heightened sense of awareness goes from its seemingly constant Yellow to Orange in a beat or two to Red. Situational awareness is something we teach in firearms instruction at every opportunity.

The SUV is running. Someone is in the driver's seat. He looks to be smoking. The window's open about a third of the way. As I exit my vehicle and start toward the building, I take another glance toward the parked vehicle, and see a rangy-looking dude coming out the front door of my building. He spots me and increases his pace as he heads toward me. His arms start flying around oddly, and he is yelling, "I am here to teach you a lesson! Stay out of people's business or it will go bad for you!" and with that he drops his head and rushes me!

I go in an instant from Red to Black. I am in the fight! Completely caught off-guard by this wild man charging at me, all I have time for is to turn toward him and square myself up. He flings his arms wide and drops his head, coming in like a skinny little linebacker. I drop my right foot back for stability just before he makes contact. I crouch as he plows into me. I can smell the rancidness of his person, combined with the heavy cigarette stench of a chain-smoker.

My rear foot slides away on the blacktop as my leather dress shoes can't find purchase. My right heel strikes the curb and I go over on my back onto the wide lawn, banging my head off the grassy but packed earth, which rings my bell and disorients me. Blows are raining down on my unprotected face and head as I regain my awareness. My arms come up and over my face and head, blocking his punches. I bridge my hips up and forward to push him off balance. The damp earth is seeping into my suit coat and shirt, and the back of my head is wet.

The SUV horn locks on full blast. I hear the engine racing... Before I can wrap up one of his arms and then trap his ankle to roll him over and come up in the guard position, he springs wide to the side and off of me. He bounces up like a rabbit, breaking contact, and bolts toward the now reversing SUV. He opens the passenger door, climbs in, and off they go down the drive at a high rate of speed.

Noel is running through the parking lot as I am rolling over to get up.

"What the fuck was that?" she screams as she gets closer.

"No fucking clue at all!" I am rubbing the back of my head from having it bounced off the damp earth. Touching my face to check the damage from the punches, my hand comes away bloody from a split lip. I spit blood and saliva into the grass. Gazing off after the vehicle, I see it makes a left turn onto the four-lane, heading south toward the interstate.

"Did you happen to get that plate number?" I ask.

"No. I was trying from the office, out the window, but no front plate... all I saw was a blue number over a white background when I looked as they sped away." Changing her tone, Noel asks, "Are you alright?"

"I think so. Just never been jumped before. Didn't even have time to get ready for it. Squirrely little fucker just came running across the parking lot screaming at me, something about teaching me a lesson."

Noel asks, "Boss, you been chasing skirts?"

"Not me! No way!" I respond. "Not sure what the fuck he was after. I think Michigan is a blue over white license plate. I can't remember having any clients up there and even if I did, I'm not sure why they would send someone to rough me up and not tell me."

Noel says, "He said the same thing to me, that he was here 'to teach the boss a lesson' or something like that." As we walk toward the back door, she asks, "Could this be about that thing you are doing for FinCEN?"

"Oh fuck... I hadn't even thought of that. What would an Indian guy from this little town be doing hiring muscle from Michigan four hours away?

I would think it could be that insurance fraud investigation I am working on with the security company."

"Boss, when I came running out the front door, that driver slammed on the horn and started reversing backward. I was sure he was going to plow you both over! Freaked me out!"

"I heard the horn and the engine growl, but I was preoccupied with wrapping that little fucker up. I was in the thick of it. Being threat-fixated can get you killed. Just glad they were not here to do any real damage. If the driver had joined in it would have gone very badly for me."

We enter the building and walk into the kitchen to pour some coffee. "So what is going on with the guy from FinCEN and the Nimbalkars?" Noel asks.

"Nothing really. I had to go back and ask them some more questions as Philip Daniels requested. I am sure by the questions they have to know that I am suspicious of something in their business dealings. Though Deepti's body language indicated surprise at the questions, Rajesh just sat very still, listening. But he seems so harmless in his canary yellow sneakers and matching watch, I can't imagine him ordering this type of shit." Filling my coffee mug, I say, "I am going to give FinCEN a call and see what Mr. Daniels has to say about this little warning."

I walk across the hall and close the door to my office. Setting my coffee down on my desk, I go into my private bathroom to see what damage has been done to my face. It is never as bad as it feels—the human body, especially the head, can take a pretty good beating. Looks like some blows landed on my forehead. A couple of welts are already rising. My lower lip is bleeding through my goatee. The red blood mixing with the grey and black beard hair, having dripped down onto my dress shirt, makes it look far worse than it is.

I snatch a couple tissues from the box and dab my lip. My hands are shaking. Fuuuck! This is total bullshit! Getting attacked at my office by some drugheads!

If they can get to me so easily, they can certainly get to my family. We all live within twenty minutes of my office, different directions mostly, but still close enough.

I drop the bloody tissue into the open bowl of the toilet and hit the flush handle. Backtracking to my desk, sucking on the blood flowing from my lip, I retrieve my cell phone to send out a family text. "Hey I just got knocked down in my office parking lot and punched in the face a few times by some tweaker drughead. Dark SUV with Michigan plates and a second guy driving. Not sure what it has to do with me yet. Don't have any pissed off clients. Could be about the Insurance Investigation job I am working surveillance for or something else. Just keep your head up and watch out for anything sketchy."

I no sooner hit the send button than my phone vibrates with my wife Sofia's picture. I take a deep breath and drop down in my desk chair. I pick up the phone and with as much cheer as I can muster say, "Hi Babe! I met some of your people today." That's my inside joke about her job as a drug counselor. Well ... Adults with Addictions as she would say.

I cover the events of being jumped and punched in the head to Sofia in as much detail as I feel makes sense. I am sure, when I get home tonight, I will need to provide a greater accounting of the events in detail that she is sure to draw out of me. My cell vibrates with a text message from my daughter Libby. I will need to remember to respond to her.

As I finish the call from Sofia, my desk intercom system buzzes and SAM's voice comes through. She must have just come back from her lunch. She tells me I have a call from one of my many investment clients.

"I can't deal with that at the moment," I say in a somewhat pleading tone. "I have another call I need to make. Let him know I will call him back later today."

I read Libby's text message. She is so sweet, all love and sorry for your pain and she will keep on the lookout for dirtbags! Hard to raise your daughters to be independent and tough without scaring the shit out of them. So, I basically try to scare the shit out of anyone they come in contact with. Boyfriends just love me! The Puddle of Mud song drifts through my mind, "maybe I'm the one, that's the paranoid psycho ..."

Again using my cell phone, I speed dial Mr. Philip Daniels. The switchboard picks up, and I am placed on hold. I wait, and I wait (and I wait)— nearly five minutes goes by before my call is picked up. "Philip Daniels here," he states with that authoritative voice he uses as a weapon.

"Hey, it's Trevor McCowen," I spit out, continuing my dialog in a staccato not unlike a warranty disclaimer on a TV car advertisement. "So, this drugged out dude jumps me in my office parking lot a little bit ago! Says, 'I need to teach you a lesson!' then bum rushes me, knocks me down and pummels my head and face. When my secretary came running out, his buddy pulled the car up and the dude jumped off me like a jackrabbit and off they sped!" I pause, waiting for some type of response. I get nothing. "It was a late model SUV with Michigan plates. Well, blue over white plates, pretty sure that is Michigan." I finish up, almost out of breath.

"Sounds more like a pissed off client or boyfriend than a creditable threat."

The fucker! Figures he would not take this seriously. I skip over the bullshit deflection and cut right to it. "What do your friends at the NSA say about Raj's cell phone use?"

"I have not involved any other agencies at this point. Still seems early to be burning up their time and manpower when we clearly have a case already with Raj," Daniels states.

"This is a joke, right? You're conducting a federal investigation with limited knowledge of the players? Help me understand that."

Philip slows down his line of commentary as though he is speaking to a child. "Listen Trevor—everything is budgets, manpower, and money. All of it needs to be justified before it gets spent or used. Federal agencies or township cops, it's the same everyplace you go." He continues with, "FinCEN is not one of the sexy three-letter agencies that get all the PR and glory. We develop these cases on a shoestring, minimal leads, just like how we found this case with Raj. And if the reward and the budget don't equal out, we will let him fall through the cracks. We can't chase every single case of money laundering that occurs." His voice hardens. "I can unleash the gates of Hell, and bring the full fury of multiple federal agencies down on a true threat to our country, but you absolutely must bring me something of greater value than we are seeing right now. Some evidence of large-scale money laundering or a link to international mobs or terrorists. Without that, this will remain a local team effort with minimal support."

"Hey!" I say. "How is this *my job* to find more evidence? Just because my client is maybe into some tax evasion doesn't mean it's my sole responsibility to build a case for you!"

"Even on a local level we should be able to get a warrant for his cell phone records, at least build a pattern of numbers he is talking to."

"I still say this Michigan rough-up is connected," I say softly.

"Okay, Trevor. I will give you that. Let me get that warrant for Raj's cell phone use and see what other numbers he is connecting with. It may take a week or more for that to get through all the local channels and the cell phone company."

"Damn ... it's nothing like they show on TV. No one is walking paperwork around to judges' houses at night, interrupting dinner hours just so we can move forward with our case?"

He actually chuckles. A little. "No, real life is just not like that. Everything takes far more time to get done. Hang in there and stick to the task at hand."

CHAPTER 30
COUSIN TALK, PART TWO

Raj and his cousin Girish from India are playing the assassins game again, and talking through the video gaming message system.

Girish says, "Thanks for sending over the *paisa* for my new kicks! When I come over can I make some fat smacks of Benjamins you talk about?"

Raj types out LOL in the reply message. "No, no, cousin! They are 'stacks,' not 'smacks.' You need to get it right or they will laugh you off the street."

"Well, I just want to sell like you and make *paisa* and buy cool stuff!" Girish answers. "If I can get my father to bring me over to the US when he and his friends come to look at buildings and farm equipment to buy, can I sell with you?"

Raj says, "You can sell, but not out of The Tunnel. You will have to find your own spot to sell. I will keep some of your sales money to cover my expenses of having you." Raj starts to think of how much he could make if his cousin starts selling his product also, and he is making a cut of all sales.

They talk for a while about the stuff they will buy with all the money they will make—the latest video gaming console and *lots and lots* of games.

Raj will be asking soon for more product from Chance. He will need to vouch for his cousin and make sure he turns in the right amount of money for the product he buys.

The two of them working together could really add a lot of money to the pile Raj has been amassing in the furnace room of the Q-Mart. He has money hidden at home as well, but much more is hidden at the store.

Raj says, "I did not know your family farmed."

"I don't think that my *abba* farms, but I think some of the men coming with him do. I think he is looking at a building or a business to buy. He had better get me travel papers or I will not be able to come to visit. I ask him most every day about it!"

Raj, setting the scope of his sniper rifle on a new target in the game, smiles and nods. He hopes Girish can make it over too. The only thing better than money is making a ton more of it.

CHAPTER 31

BRING HIM TO ME

Mr. Philip Daniels is sitting in the Atlas Corp. building meeting with Face and me.

"So," he begins, "we have compiled a list of the phone numbers that Rajesh Nimbalkar is contacting. One of them links back to a guy named Chance Richardson—Ohio resident the past six months. Drives a late model Camaro. Current address is 1215 Washington Street SW."

I come back with, "Not a bad part of town, but certainly near the border-line. Housing is rather cheap and you can be about anyplace in the city in less than ten minutes. What have you learned from this guy Chance's phone use?"

"Not a thing. We don't even know if he is really connected yet. I can't just get phone records without warrants and warrants require evidence of illicit activity."

"So, what do you want us to do with this Chance guy?"

"Bring him to me."

"You are asking us to snatch a dude off the streets? That is a clear felony. Are you covering us for that?"

There is a very long pause before Mr. Daniels says, "Use your power of persuasion that you are so good at, and have him meet with me. I want to look into his eyes and see what he knows about Rajesh's operation, because he obviously has one."

Face chimes in with, "How about this ... We take you to him. My team clears a path for you and stands security for a meet and greet between you two. Say ... at his house, early some morning when he is still groggy and not awake."

As he stands to leave, Mr. Daniels says, "Make it happen and keep me in the loop."

Once Face and I are alone and the door is closed, he says, "You are right. That guy's a fucking prick. He was going to let us snatch that dude up and then take the fall for kidnapping. That is some truly hard-core shit to try and pass off."

"We have an address and a photo from the BMV. Let's put a plan together on this so-called meet and greet you so graciously offered to make happen," I answer.

With the help of Google Maps and the County Auditor website we have a basic image of the home—square footage, number of floors, placement of some windows and doors. With Google Street View we have surrounding homes and a six-month-old overhead view of the area. Seems like a quiet enough residential section, right in between the two main routes that run through downtown.

We decide on four vehicles—two on either street to literally block a lane of traffic in front of the property and two on the street that runs behind the house, in case he bolts out the back. Lead drivers with the vehicles and one other operator from each ride will act as a security officer. The four security officers will make their way to the front and back doors, and, with radios, coordinate entry. Once the subject is secure, we can have Mr. Prick and this Chance guy have their little meeting while we all stand security.

Face continues with, "Blackout gear, handguns and soft armor only, very low profile. I will have Mr. Daniels sign a contract with Atlas before we are a go. A ... I want protection in case something goes wrong and B ... it would be cool to get paid by a federal agency that we are doing work for!"

I respond with, "Knowing your luck, it will be direct deposit and not a hard check that you can make a photo copy of that would read Financial Crimes Unit US Treasury!" We both laugh as we conclude the meeting. Doing Cool Guy Shit is all we care about and having proof of it makes it even better.

Face says, "You can't be in on this little escapade."

I nod my head. "As much as it will kill me to sit this one out, I get it. No sense getting my cover blown with Atlas *or* FinCEN. Since this guy is connected somehow to Raj, I need to stay in the background." Shrugging, I add, "At least one of us is getting paid for their services on this job."

"Really? They aren't paying you?"

"Nope. Not a dime. My home office says it is 'our honor to assist the Financial Crimes Department of the US Treasury.'" These home office people have no clue how much time I am burning up on this case. And personally, I still don't see how it is my issue or even that my client's family are in any way terrorists or money launderers."

Face says, "One thing I have learned in the years of investigative work that I have done—nothing is as it seems in life. You truly do not know what is in the heart of a man until he's pushed to the limit."

CHAPTER 32

MEET AND GREET

Two days later, sitting in my Tahoe in an abandoned parking lot six blocks west of the two streets Atlas have blocked off, things are about to get interesting. The two Atlas teams are about to make entry into Chance Richardson's home so that Mr. Daniels of FinCEN can "look deep into his eyes" and determine if he is part of the money laundering and potential terrorist activities that he has spent months chasing after.

The predawn assessment team has completed a drive-by, and confirmed that the only vehicle in the driveway is a bright yellow Camaro—the car Chance drives, which is listed with the BMV. The color is different, but that is not uncommon with older vehicles.

I have my radio tuned to Atlas's activities channel, and I hear T-1—the Bravo Team leader—call out that he is in position at the back door of the property.

Few people I know can work a pick set like T-1. It would literally take me fifteen minutes and a ton of swearing to get a dead bolt open, but he seems to have the gift of a deft touch. In literally seconds he could be through most any key set on the market.

I sit here envisioning the events: T-1 will get the door open, the support man will be first through the door, T-1 will be the number two man. Their job is to clear the kitchen, dining room, and living room. If by then Alpha Team has not gotten the front door open, Bravo Team will unlock it from the inside.

Bravo Team will hold the first floor, while Alpha Team moves up the stairs and makes contact with the package (that's Chance). Once he is secured, Mr. Daniels will be brought in for the conversation. All very cloak and dagger. Should be enough to put the fear of God into Chance and get some type of information out of him.

I know what you're thinking: Is this legal? Depends on how you look at it. Atlas has a signed contract with Daniels to secure a face-to-face meeting with Chance Richardson. When investigating federal crimes, law enforcement seems to have a great deal of leeway. None of the information could be used in court, but you can still learn a lot by shaking a guy up.

I sit in silence, listening to the radio callouts. Bravo Team needs to let Alpha Team in the front door.

Alpha's door man is going to catch hell for needing to be let in.

Once the front door is open, all is quiet as they clear the balance of the home, including the basement. It is a good six minutes before I hear the call-out that the package is secure and it is good to bring in Daniels.

In my mind's eye I am watching it unfold. Chance on the side of the bed, flex-cuffed hands behind his back, groggy, confused as to what is happening. We had the Atlas teams wear black face scarves so only their eyes show, no patches on their tactical gear—all very official-looking.

Mr. Daniels, in his finely cut suit, will stride purposefully into the room, get up in Chance's face, and grill him with questions on his involvement and what he knows.

Ten minutes later, the radio crackles to life with a simple statement—"All clear"—and it is over. I drop the shift into drive and slowly roll forward to ease onto the street. I feed gas to the V-8 engine and move into traffic, heading east toward Atlas's office.

Forty-five minutes later, Face and I are sitting across from Mr. Daniels, discussing the morning's successful "meet and greet" with Chance Richardson.

I have not bothered to tell anyone that I was sitting a few blocks down the street from all the fun. Face and I want to talk about how the teams worked and moved, but we know that Mr. Daniels has other plans.

I start with, "What did you find out?"

"It would seem that the only solid information Chance has is that he is providing pot to Rajesh at the Q-Mart, and he is selling it a joint at a time through the beverage tunnel."

My mouth is hanging open as I take in this information. I stammer, "Well, that must be why his mom said his sales were up so much."

Mr. Daniels nods. "And that fits with the bank's statement that Rajesh was trying to deposit a large sum of cash and their taking note of his fancy new purchases."

"Did Richardson say who his supplier is?" Face asks.

"No. Just that he receives shipments out of Detroit," Daniels states. "I will pass this onto DEA and it will work its way down to local departments who will make a case against Rajesh and Chance and hopefully make inroads with his Detroit supplier. There is just so much of this going on it's difficult to run every lead down and make formal charges. Seems like the money laundering is just Rajesh's dumb ass being obvious and sloppy and there's no clear connection to terrorism, so this case is quickly coming to an end for me. With just one attempted deposit, we will hold this information until DEA can make a case against him and use it for leverage. No need to waste it as a stand-alone case."

"As fun as this has been, am I out of the investigation as well?" I ask.

"Yes. I will notify your Home Office Compliance Department that you have been a big help." He emphasizes *big* the same way you would speak to a child about helping. The guy is still a fucking prick!

"Who are you after next?" I ask.

"We may poke around Detroit a little bit to be sure nothing funnels back overseas. We will keep tabs on Rajesh's cousin, this Girish, and Rajesh's uncle as well. but mostly I will just wait for the next lead to come in."

And with that said, Mr. Daniels stands and heads for the door. No one shakes hands anymore, so we all just sort of nod to each other as he makes his way out.

Face and I sit back down, and T-1 comes through the conference room door to join us. He is excited with the morning's work and wants to hear all about the details.

We spend forty-five minutes reviewing after-action and hot washing the details. Alpha Team's door man needs to brush up on his lock-picking skills.

As the meeting is finishing up, I ask Face how much he charged FinCEN for this morning's "meet and greet." He laughs and says that he heavily *over-*charged them for man hours, and that—Big Man that he thinks he is—Daniels signed the invoice like it wasn't an issue at all.

"Be sure to save that for posterity!" I say.

CHAPTER 33

FOLLOWING THE LIMPER

Sitting in a rental car a quarter mile up the road from the subject's house, I am waiting on the trigger for him to leave the residence. I have my monocular pressed against my eye, watching for the front door to open.

I have a cool little smartphone attachment for the monocular so that I can video-record the subject from a distance with reasonable enough clarity for identification. This, coupled with the front and rear dash cameras, assist in making my rolling office a solid witness for court to derail this asshat's desire to defraud the insurance company.

I've been doing close follow on him for some time now, vehicle and foot. We have some evidence of him not limping but need to get so much of it that he agrees to simply drop the case. The client does not wish to spend the money it will take lawyers to go to court—he would rather spend a quarter of that money on investigation. I think our hourly rate is high for this type of work—I can't imagine an attorney charging four times that rate for litigation.

The Baofeng radio crackles to life. I have the local law-enforcement channel programmed in to alert me early in case someone calls in a suspicious vehicle that fits my vehicle's description. Gives me time to move off before local law enforcement can arrive and starts asking me questions I don't wish to answer.

I am not doing anything wrong or illegal—there's just no reason to call attention to myself with flashing lights and a pat down from law enforcement that the subject might see and remember.

> "447 to control—Male DOA"
> Control: "Copy"
> 447: "Control, the house is registered to Jamie, male, Banner"
> Control: "Is the caller there?"
> 447: "Umm yes, he is hanging out in the driveway."
> Control: "Do you need anything?"
> "410 to 447 direct, I will be there in three!"
> 447: "Copy"

The radio never gives the full story. I would guess a drug overdose. The first officer (447) sounded very upset about having to find and check the body. Of course, no one wants a DOA. Don't know if the caller is the homeowner, or if this is a guest or family member. Drugs make strange bedfellows. People seem to sell their very soul for that shit. I simply can't understand taking a drug that you will become addicted to the very first time you use it.

My wife Sofia, an Adults with Addiction counselor, deals with this rampant crisis every single day. I truly do not know how she does it—hearing their stories and excuses. So few ever make it to sobriety and turn their lives around.

I normally hear stories about overdose leading to death, patients running away from treatment and hiding out and binging on a wider variety of drugs, oftentimes leading to their death. Sofia has had two clients straight up murdered in the past eighteen months—one for steeling $75,000 in cash from her dealer and the other for not having enough drugs to share with the other people in the car.

Patients are tested twice a week and some come in with drug levels in excess of what the human body is supposed to be able to withstand, and yet they somehow manage to keep moving. Many are great at hiding that they are higher than a kite!

The sun has set and the surrounding neighborhood is growing darker. Lights are coming on around me. The radio remains silent. The front porch light flicks on at the subject's house. The door opens and a triangle of light spills out onto the front walk. The fraudster comes limping out the door, cane in one hand to steady his movements.

Using the smartphone connection to the monocular I take video of his progress to the car. I can't start my vehicle till he is moving. I am pretty sure he is set to come out from his road onto the one that intersects the parallel road I am sitting on so I can fall in behind him.

Once he is focused on getting his car backed into the side street, I start my vehicle and drift forward toward the stop sign, and he turns right, the opposite direction of travel I expected him to go. Well, that is the way of it in surveillance—plan and plan all day long, just to have your plans dashed on the rocks of reality.

As I wait at the stop sign for traffic to pass, two cars get between us, which is even better for tailing someone. Having it get dark is also a big help.

He continues his travels through the little town, passing traffic lights and stop signs, while cars move in and out around us. I have been directly behind him for the past three lights. Time to break off so he does not get suspicious of a follow.

I make the next left turn into a neighborhood. Everything is laid out in grid formation. I roll to the next stop sign and make a quick right turn so that I am parallel, one street over, from his route of travel. He will have traffic lights and I will have stop signs. He is on a main street and I'm on residential side street.

Four blocks up I am sitting for a little too long at a stop sign, waiting to catch a glimpse of him going through the green light. Nothing, and still nothing. A car rolls up behind me and I choose to make the turn and head back toward the main street. At least now if I pull out behind him, he will not think it's a follow.

My light is still red, and there's no sign of his vehicle in the traffic passing through the light or oncoming. Shit ... how did I lose him? This is when a two-car tail works far better, but the budget would not permit it.

Fuck! If I lose him tonight, I will need to do this again next week when he heads out to meet friends and have some drinks. You only get so many chances to nail a guy, and it is beginning to look like I blew this one.

I make a right turn on red and head back the way he should be coming. There ... a block up and over he is getting gas at the service station. Wonderful! I roll past and turn around a half block up and wait at the side of the road in an empty parking spot for him to finish up. I am not worried about my head lights still being on and just sitting here—there is enough local activity I will be unnoticed.

He finishes pumping. Shit ... no cane! Before I can reach for the camera and monocular, he shifts around with a limp and a gimp and uses the door as support to get back into the car.

I effortlessly roll in a safe distance behind him, following him up the onramp to the four-lane interstate. Thirty-five minutes later he exits the highway, turns left at the top of the ramp, and continues down the busy undivided four lane road packed with restaurants, truck stops, gas stations, and strip clubs.

A half mile up the road, Limper turns into the local casino and horse race track. I stay wide of his direction of travel in the parking lot and slide to a stop against a curb, shutting down my ride and getting the camera and monocular ready.

I can see clearly the section he parks in but there are so many large pickup trucks and SUVs that he is lost in the mix. I hit record and wait for him to pop out into the clear of the parking lot heading toward the front doors of the casino.

Sure as shit, there he is, moving through the parking lot, *no visible limp or cane to be seen.* I am so glad to be rolling digital on this. I will be uploading the footage tonight with my report to Face at Atlas Corp. so he can forward it on to the client. The dude is almost *skipping* he is moving so fast.

I see no reason to follow him in—I can't get any better footage than this! Of course, it is nighttime, and I am a hundred-plus yards away, taking video through an optical lens. I put the vehicle into drive and look for a place to park. I had better try to get some footage in good lighting from inside.

Close walking surveillance is a different animal than vehicle. Same principal, though—don't get blown, but it is harder not to stare at the person when you are in close proximity. And getting video can be a little tricky.

Once parked, I strip off my handgun and knife. The casino has a very strict no weapons policy. If I was working close personal protection, I would have called ahead and arranged to be permitted in with a gun, but at this short notice and not working for a client I am sure they would balk at letting me in with a gun tonight. No worry...this is just a close follow insurance scam job. Nothing dangerous.

The second floor has a bar–restaurant overlooking the casino floor. The horse track is underneath the restaurant, but there is no racing tonight, so he should be in the casino someplace.

I order a coffee with cream from a waitress and place a twenty-dollar bill on the table I have chosen, which sort of lets her know I will take care of her. She moves off to take a dinner order from a couple a few tables away.

I can easily expense this coffee off for this job. Can't hit it hard, but twenty bucks won't be fussed over.

I scan the floor below, looking for Limper in earnest. I spot him sitting at a slot machine. Well, maybe this is not such a great idea—hard to get video of him moving around if he is just sitting static.

As I wait for my coffee I scroll through social media on my phone, which is a good way to keep the phone upright and ready to hit video mode when he moves, and it permits me to look lost in my mindless phone, being bored and doing nothing of importance. Coffee shops and smartphones have made surveillance a simpler game. No more hiding behind a magazine or newspaper.

Time passes. After I finish my second coffee, I can see him still sitting at the same machine. He looks to be texting on his phone. He looks behind him and waves an arm in the air, and a guy and a woman bounce up to his spot and start talking with animated gestures.

I scroll through the phone apps to the camera and bring up video. I press record and zoom in just enough to get them all in the frame. He slides off the stool and the three of them walk—his limp completely gone—toward the stairs, heading for the bar–restaurant where I am located. I follow their progress through the phone screen, and as soon as they hit the stairs to come up, I close the phone down, place my coffee cup on the twenty-dollar bill, get up and move away from them toward the bathroom. Time to break and roll. Once I come out of the bathroom, I will need to keep my head down and simply move out with purpose.

While I am washing my hands the door opens, and in walks no-longer-the-Limper. Well, fuck me. Not what I'd expected, but anything is possible in surveillance. I grab a paper towel from the basket on the counter and dry my hands. He actually grunts a greeting, which I return with "Hey" while moving toward the door.

As I pull it open, he says, "Do I know you?"

Without looking back I say, "I doubt it" and keep moving away.

Well, that will not look good in my report! Cover blown by the subject. Face will understand it. He has worked enough surveillance to know this shit can happen. At least we finally have the proof we need to finish up this fraud case with the insurance company investigator.

All things considered, it was a damn good night.

CHAPTER 34

STAKEOUT

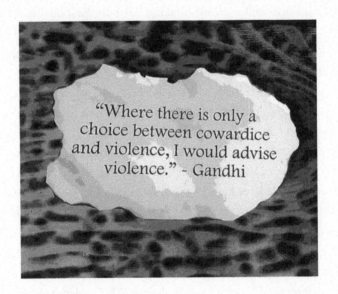

"Where there is only a choice between cowardice and violence, I would advise violence." ~ Gandhi

Sitting in my dark blue Tahoe halfway up the block on East 89th Street, in a small parking lot with delivery vans all around me for cover, I am watching one of the Main Campus buildings of Get Well, Inc.

There is really no good street parking in the area, so the company provides lots of nearby multilevel parking garages.

T-1 is sitting in his silver Ford F-150, stationed on Carnegie Avenue, in a maintenance turnout, covering vehicles traveling on East 96th Street. Tiger Lily is on East 102nd in one of the few standard parking lots. His two-door orange vehicle blends well with the cityscape in which we are working.

Our hand-held radios are all tuned to Atlas International Security Corp. for team communication and Cleveland PD is set for listen mode only. It is always good to hear what is going on around you, if for no other reason than to break the monotony of static surveillance.

We do a general comms and status check every thirty minutes, which breaks up the night and keeps us from dozing off. I even get out of the Tahoe at one point and take a short walk around the area.

There is always some level of traffic—this is a city by definition—and this location is pretty much in the middle of it, with housing all around, and many of its streets provide local lanes of travel for people living in the area.

The hand-held radio crackles to life with the local police department dispatch callout:

"Unit 87, alarm drop at 209 Golden Avenue."

I glance at the dashboard clock. It's 12:11 am.

Dispatch repeats: "Unit 87, alarm drop at 209 Golden Avenue, motion in master and smoke alarm."

"87 in route."

"Copy."

"Control to 87."

87: "Go ahead."

Control: "Do you want fire?"

87: "No. I will check out the site and advise."

After a period of silence:

"87 to control."

Control: "Go ahead."

87: "Check, secure, clear, I am 35, out."

As Control responds with the standard "Copy," I glance at the dashboard time again. Now it's 12:17 am. In my mind I try to see how the officer handled this six-minute call. Two minutes away max with traffic lights for which he would have only slowed down. Left car running and walked up to the door closest to the driveway. Turned the knob, knocked, moved around the house to the back, checking windows, alarm must have reset or got turned off. Made contact with the homeowner who tripped the alarm. Saw his driver's license and moved off and rolled out.

Tiger Lily breaks the radio on Atlas Corp. "It is so frustrating not knowing how that stuff ends! All we ever hear is limited information."

T-1 responds with, "At least it was not for a suspicious F-150 or Tahoe. I have had to leave a really good surveillance spot a time or two because someone called the cops on my parked vehicle."

I add, "It's always surprising to me what goes on within a few miles of our day-to-day lives and we are none the wiser for it. It's as though I live in a vacuum, I swear. This job has really opened my eyes to the public around me, and they are sort of a hot mess! I've listened to some crazy stuff over the airwaves."

Time passes. The dashboard clock reads 2:37 am. I reach for the coffee thermos on my seat and unscrew the lid. As I start to turn the plug, my radio crackles to life.

Tiger Lily says, "I have a very slow-moving four-door car heading north on East 102nd. Older model, dark blue in color."

T-1 responds, "Keep an eye on them and report as long as you can see them." He then swings out and comes up around the block toward them.

"Be sure your dash cam is on so we can get a plate number and facial as you roll past," I say with a bit of excitement in my voice.

I drop the Tahoe into drive and ease out into the empty street. I will roll up to Route 20 and come down East 105th. I make a fifty–fifty guess that I will also pass this car. East 102nd deadends at a T intersection prior to Route 20. It's worth a shot, and it will keep me awake.

As I am coming up to the intersection with East 100th Street, I see a dark-colored four-door car passing through the intersection after coming off a stop sign. I key my radio. "T-1. Any visual?"

He responds with, "Negative."

I say, "This may be him in front of me. I am going to follow, traveling north on East 100th."

T-1 answers, "I will head your way and back you up."

Tiger Lily chimes in with, "I can head that way too."

I say, "No. Hold your position. We are too far for you to catch up."

I make the turn onto East 100th Street. I can see the car up the block, his right-hand turn signal is on, and I am thinking he is going to turn onto Route 322 and head east into the sketchy part of town. As I get closer, he turns into the parking lot of the local drug store and goes inside. I relay this info to T-1, and pull in behind the car. I position my vehicle so the dash cam gets a clear view of both the license plate and the front door so, when the subject exits, I should be able to get a clear visual of this guy who rolled through our net.

This could just be some dude picking up diapers or a prescription, but it fits our profile, so we need to keep on it, knowing that we will have more nobodies than somebodies to chase.

T-1 pulls into the lot, parking right next to the car in question. He gets out, ambles up to the drug store door, and goes in. He is always scruffy faced, and stubble-headed, with a fair amount of grey coming in. He is in his usual work pants, leather work boots, and a simple graphic T-shirt. Dressed like this, he blends in almost anywhere—the typical working man stopping to buy something on his way home. Hell, he may even actually buy something he needs. His phone is in his ear, talking to no one I'm sure. His video camera is running and he's going to get good clear, up close images of this guy.

Sure as hell, he is standing in line behind the subject, a gallon of milk in his left hand, phone in his right. He rotates around, like he is looking behind him, taking video of the guy checking out.

As the blue car backs up, I write down the plate number just in case the dash cam does not get a clear image. I get out and cross the lot. T-1 holds the door as I walk in, and I say, like he's a stranger, "Hey ... thanks, man."

He continues to his truck and I head for the chip aisle, thinking a bag of popcorn and some candy would go well with tonight's activities.

Back in the Tahoe, I hit the radio. "Good job on the 'walk up,' T-1. You are a master at close work. We got clear visuals and vehicle tags we can run, if there are any broken windows in the morning."

When the dash clock reads 5:00 am, I cue the mic with, "This task and detail is done for the day. Head home, gentlemen." I get one "Roger out" and one "Hard copy" in return. I drop the Tahoe into gear and rolled out of the small lot, heading up to Route 322, to head west toward I-90 South toward home and some sleep before a full afternoon of meetings at the office.

CHAPTER 35
TELL RAJ TO GET OUT

Rolling down Market Street, heading east, back toward my office from Atlas HQ, I just cannot get my most recent meeting with Mr. Philip Daniels of FinCEN out of my mind—the forced "meet and greet" with the mid-level drug dealer Chance Richardson, his potential involvement in money laundering or terrorism with Rajesh, and how Mr. FinCEN Agent Man was going to turn his findings over to the local DEA for investigation. It is just too much for me to deal with. I feel like I betrayed my client's trust.

It haunts me. Rajesh's parents have been investment clients of mine since he was in grade school. If his dad were still alive, Rajesh would never be selling pot in the drive-through tunnel. The kid is clearly just misdirected and doesn't know how much trouble he could get into.

I am certainly happy that Mr. Daniels is not planning to pursue money laundering charges against Rajesh any time soon. And with my high confidence that he has no ties to terrorists, I feel like it would be nice to just see this entire mess go away.

I am still so frustrated that FinCEN and Daniels were able to use the USA PATRIOT Act to force me into helping them investigate my clients. Now that they are clearly not criminals—well … at least not terrorists or money launderers—I am thinking about the moral and legal nuances of what Rajesh *is* involved in. Pot is legal in so many states already. I know, I am just self-justifying his actions, but I don't want my clients to have any more pain, especially over an impulsive decision to sell some pot.

It feels so good to be free of the federal oversight of Mr. Daniels. He was such a prick and hardass all the time. No appreciation for anyone's efforts— just results. I need to stay off his radar forever!

Now that I am released from his oversight and there is no threat to National Security, I can tell Rajesh to get out of the pot business before the local DEA rolls him up and destroys his and his mom's lives. His uncle would be crushed to know what his nephew is doing.

Before I even realize what I'm doing, I find myself sitting in the line for the Q-Mart drive-through tunnel. Oh, fuck! Maybe I should just keep my mouth shut and let this play out naturally, which would mean Rajesh getting rolled up in some local drug sting and crushing his family. Or, worse yet, getting flipped into being a drug informant and being at the mercy of the great War on Drugs.

And there he is, looking at me, recognition setting in, a slight smile crossing his eyes and face. "Hey, Mr. McCowen!" No matter how many times I tell him to call me Trevor, he always uses my surname.

Before I can think up what to say, I hear myself blurt out, "The cops are onto you, Rajesh! Stop selling pot now and you may get away without being caught! They know about Chance!"

His face goes slack, like he's just seen a ghost. He stands there, staring at me, and all I can think to do is drive off. I let my foot off the brake and the Tahoe eases forward out the end of The Tunnel.

I wait to slip into traffic, stuck at a red light, anxious to head for home. I have had enough of this day. I need some quiet time at the farm. Maybe watching the sheep graze in the pasture will wash this day off me, like a cool spring rain.

As I continue to wait on the traffic light, I glance in the rearview mirror and there is Rajesh, still awestruck, looking at my vehicle pulling away. The next car in line gently toots its horn and Rajesh is snapped out of it. He walks over to the drive and I read his lips. "Give me a minute," he says, stepping into the cash payment booth.

He yanks his phone out of his front pocket and I see him texting. I'm pretty sure the target of the text is Chance, and it says something like, "We need to meet. I need help."

Rajesh is still shaken up as he attends to the waiting customer as I pull into traffic and out of his line of sight.

CHAPTER 36

THE BEAST WITHIN

It was a mad dash, the day I met both my Beast within and my old friend Death.

I have found in my lifetime a startling anomaly. Deep, deep inside the very essence of Self, there lives a being, and I have truly known him to be a Beast. This knowledge is extremely shocking and frightening to a Christian man, raised on the word of God, taught the Bible and to love my fellow humans—to learn forgiveness, honor, and so much more.

I often wonder if perhaps this Beast is my *true* Self, and this other me—this me that walks around serving the world's needs—perhaps he is the alien, or, as the Bible states, "The spirit of God who lives in you."

Perhaps our evolution from Cro-Magnon to Homo sapiens to this Modern Man that I am today, dressed in a blue suit, a crisp white shirt, and black shoes is all because of this Spirit of God that lives within me. So that when I practice my religious belief and call upon my God, that he answers ... regardless of the religion that I am born and raised with, converted to, or forced to wear like a coat by some dictator. Perhaps this alien spirit that lives within us is truly changing us, molding us ever so slowly over the millennia of time and space to become something greater than the Beast this Spirit first encountered upon coming to Earth so many thousands and thousands of year ago.

Back then, the Beast often would have won in the struggle of Spirit versus Beast, for he was much more pronounced and far stronger than that Still Small Voice that lives within us.

But all things change—ever so slowly. Thousands of years of change is still change. Until the here and now of today, we are what we are and we strive for so much more.

My thinking must not be new or even original. All thoughts are old— very, very old. It is only the individual who feels their thoughts are fresh and new. It reminds me of the William Blake poem, "The Tyger":

> Tyger, Tyger, burning bright,
> In the forests of the night;
> What immortal hand or eye,
> Could frame thy fearful symmetry?
> In the distant deeps or skies.

Burnt the fires of thine eyes?
On what wings dare he aspire?
What the hand, dare seize the fire?

And what shoulder, & what art,
Could Twist the sinews of thy heart?
And when they heart began to beat,
What dread hand? & what dread feet?

What the hammer? What the Chain,
In what furnace was thy brain?
What the anvil? What dread gasp,
Dare its deadly terrors clasp!

When the stars threw down their spears
And the water'd heavens with their tears:
Did he smile his work to see?
Did he who made the Lamb make thee?

Tyger, Tyger burning bright,
In the forests of the night:
What immortal hand or eye,
Dare frame thy fearful symmetry?

I find that, with all poetry and even the Bible, we take the contextual parts of the poem or verse that speak to us deeply or that we can use as a weapon against others, to defend our own thoughts. With this Blake poem, it is the line, "Did he who made the Lamb make thee?" A great question to ponder when we consider that ability and ferocity of the Beast within.

The Beast is nothing new. The Irish knew of him, often referred to as the Berserker. In the heat of the battle he would emerge from each man and fight with the ferocity of ten.

General George C. Marshall, Jr. has been quoted as saying that, in war, officers must learn to control the Beast struggling at the chains that keep it locked inside of them and the men who serve beneath them.

And, should it come free, how do we, that new us, the Spirit of God that lives in us, reconcile the two as one, as Self? I think it's best expressed by Sgt. Brandi, USMC, in a letter to his Fellow Warriors. In a nutshell, Brandi says that the Beast must not be threatened, but fed. But not too much. Just enough that it is ready if you are threatened. But you must acknowledge and console it. Thank it. For your life, your survival. Then, and only then, can you control it.

My entire life I have held these beliefs to be my truth. I have shared them countless times with others in an almost religious format, even sharing my inner ideas of the alien of God living inside of us with a Baptist pastor client. At the end of my dissertation on bringing Darwin, God, aliens, and the afterlife all into a single construct, he gazed at me (I felt in disbelieve), and said, "Well, young man ..."—I am not young, he just happens to be thirty years my senior—"you have said much, some I understand and could even agree to, some goes against my upbringing and teaching. I would like for you to continue to search and ask and seek what is right for you."

Wanting desperately to have his approval, I hurriedly said, "Perhaps I am simply using the wrong words, or calling aliens and God something we ... we have just never considered them to be!"

He pushed back his chair heavily and stood. "Always seek. It is the only way you will find. And know that I love you." I shook his large warm hand and he turned and shuffled down the hallway toward the office door.

I think all of these thoughts so often and seek so deeply for an answer that oftentimes frustration appears and I must set it all aside.

My mind has been so heavily preoccupied with these random thoughts. I get that my subconscious wants me to hear something, to *know* something, but this case with FinCEN has literally swamped me, causing so much anxiety and stress; making me tired—always so very, very tired. I can hardly focus my thoughts to sort through the problems of how to obtain the hard evidence the feds want should they call on me again and to keep them from continuing to exploit me with threats of legal action and expulsion from the industry I have spent my life in and built a successful business from. One built purely on trust and often on a handshake.

All of this has been raging through my mind, keeping my lizard brain from reading the signs of threat matrix that have been projecting to me all morning. First, a phone appointment sheet from a new client I have never met, set at a location I have never been to, by my staff, who normally don't do things like this. But he stated he was a referral from a well-known attorney who has sent me very solid clients in the past, so I was not as concerned as if it was a cold introduction.

As I roll up to the three-story brick building, I notice the old stone work and balconies of the style of city housing built in the 1940s and '50s.

This building is under rehabilitation as they take the small hotel-style rooms of each floor and convert them into large, lofty condos.

My mind is having difficulty comprehending the two people on a third-floor balcony looking directly down at me—a large, dark-skinned man, with hair that waves like the ocean. And the other... Damn... that looks like my daughter Keira, who has been visiting us from her home in Wilmington, North Carolina. Shit... It *is* Keira! Just then, Keira jerks loose of the man's hold on her arm and screams, "Daddy! NOOOOO!"

As my mind tries to take all of this in, a huge, heavy *thunk* strikes the front windshield directly in front of my face. The windshield does not spiderweb like from a rock strike—this is a live round that completely obscures all visibility. The front window holds, as another round is fired into the same location. I am jerked into the realization that this is an ambush, a trap to lure me in and kill me on the spot, using my daughter as bait, and then as a red herring, to keep my focus from scanning the surroundings for threat assessment.

Today I am driving my fully armored Mercedes Benz G-280 three-door Follow Vehicle, complete with armored 60-pound hatch door on the roof above the trunk monkey seat.

My side gig as armed security doing valuable transport and executive protection made it clear that we needed solid wheels for the types of jobs we contracted to complete for jewelry stores, rare coin dealers, and the occasional politician or rich dude who wanted to show off at trendy local restaurants. As a side business it seemed strange at times even to me, but from a desire to learn as much as I can about threat protection and tactical engagement there was no equal. Not even law enforcement provided this level of Cool Guy excitement, proven by the fact that a number of our armed security team were active LE and former SWAT officers.

Later today, I am scheduled to assist a local jeweler with a high-end delivery, so I have the armored "G-Wagon" for that job, along with the pistol-caliber carbine, instead of the standard shotgun.

If I had driven my Tahoe as usual, I would most likely be dead.

Other rounds start striking the hood and the sides as the goons lose accuracy with the increased rate of fire. I roll out of the driver's seat and navigate my way to the back trunk monkey seat. Cabled to the swivel chair bolted to the floor is a bag containing my turnout gear and a Sig Sauer MPX with a seven-inch barrel and Sig suppressor. Completing this compact bag gun is the skeletal folding stock and Holosun red dot sight.

Rounds continue to strike the vehicle, truly deafening and completely unnerving. My hands are shaking as I sling my ceramic plates on and attempt to seat a 30-round 9mm magazine into the mag well. *Easy brother ... take a deep breath ... blow it out.* Having never been under direct, accurate contact I am having trouble processing all the outside stimuli.

I jam my Team Wendy ballistic helmet onto my head and snap the chin strap into place, activating the hearing protection and noise cancelation mode on the headphones. I then slide my ballistic prescription glasses onto my face, pop the NeoMag Sentry Strap magnetic sling, throw the shorty carbine around my neck and shoulder, and dig deep into the bag. My mind continues to scream, *You are out of time! That glass will not hold! Your daughter is in grave danger!* The panic is setting in, and I want to scream bloody murder. My hand closes around a large cardboard cylinder of white cover smoke.

Having only ever used this stuff in training, I am hoping it functions well in a real tactical situation! My armored vehicle is facing forward. The hatch opens to the back to be used as cover when engaging a threat behind you, but my threat is in front and to the passenger side of me. I will be overexposed pushing the sixty-pound hatch open to shoot or throw smoke.

My handgun ready at the four o'clock position and two spare mags on my belt, I am as ready as ever to roll out. As an afterthought I dial 911 on my cell and as clearly and calmly as possible state my emergency to the dispatcher. I explain with words she would understand, "Shots fired, shots fired, I am heavily armed and under attack, going in for my daughter before your boys will get here. Contact FinCEN Investigator Philip Daniels and tell him my location." As the dispatcher starts to argue against this plan—which I silently agree is not wise—I cut her off with, "I am out." I leave the phone line open, put the phone back on my belt, pull the ripcord on the smoke, drop my hand to the door handle, and realize I should have put gloves on. The smoke starts to fill the vehicle.

It is now time to go.

Pushing the 400-pound door open, I lob the smoke up and over the vehicle as hard to the left as I can toward the big Suburban they are using as cover and concealment.

I step out and roll to the back of my beautiful, dark blue G-Wagon, which continues to take rounds that produce constant, heavy thuds. Now that I'm outside I'm glad of the ear protection as the AK-47 rounds pound my vehicle. I come off the vehicle, searching through the growing smoke for a target. The 9mm shorty carbine with the suppressor is a solid, flat shooting round that will go through the doors of a vehicle but not the A or B pillars, so I will need to work the glass and find open areas to make solid hits on these goons. It is whisper quiet with the suppressor and subsonic rounds, so hopefully they will not even hear me return fire over their AK-47s.

As I work the angles from the back of my vehicle, I see a goon go empty. That fucker has put *thirty rounds* into my ride! Damn his soul to Hell! He rolls out of sight but stays up inside the window. I can see him through the back window and side window of the Suburban. I roll the carbine up so the red dot is in my right eye and send five rounds into the rear window. The first round or two shatter the glass, as the next three rounds do their job on the side window and strike the skinny little goon as he completes his reload. He drops out of sight, hopefully dead but, until that's confirmed, still a potential threat.

More rounds from the first shooter are coming in hot and fast. I hear the far window give way. Rounds are rattling around inside the cab of my G-Wagon. Fear creeps forward and I'm no longer sure I can hold this position.

My mind is a wreck, but my body is functioning under the years and years of CQB—Close Quarters Battle—training. I feel something deep within stir, like I am going to throw up, puke all over. I feel so full of emotion, I need to let it out! It wants to come out!

At that very moment the Beast steps forth in all his brutal splendor, massive in size, covered in long dark hair that waves in the air, with long heavily muscled arms, crouched slightly forward, like something out of a Conan the Barbarian book of my youth!

A round hits to my right and then another. Someone is shooting from the driver's side, out the ground floor window. I suck up against the back of the vehicle and take a breath. The Beast steps to the mouth of his cave, his head coming up as he gazes upon this world.

I snap my carbine to my shoulder, roll around the left side of my beat-to-shit G-Wagon, and into the smoke screen I have created. The smoke is thicker than I anticipated. It burns my eyes and throat. I am so glad it was not CS Gas, or I would be on the ground choking and puking to death.

The Beast bellows the ancient name of our creator, calling upon us the salvation and protection of the Lord God Almighty. I am through the smoke, staring through the red dot at goon number two, nearly barrel to barrel, my finger slipping into the trigger well and six pounds of repeated pressure sends three rounds over his barrel and into his T-Box—the first one through the nose and into the brain box, the other two into the left eye hole. The round from his AK is wide, as he was not expecting me to come straight at him through the smoke and hail of fire.

Now that I'm clear of the protective smoke, there are more rounds tearing past my head, the sound made louder by the ear pro.

The Beast lurches forward with another guttural roar at the enemy, growling curses so old they are unknown to me. I send as much hate from my suppressed carbine into that open window left of the door as I can. Pushing hard for the main entrance in front of me, my weapon comes to slide lock on an empty chamber. I let the carbine fall on its sling and snatch the Sig P320 Compact from the holster on my four o'clock, the Holosun red dot already on, floating out in front of my eyes, scanning for threats as I dynamically cross the threshold of the building.

I enter, following the open door hinged to the right, and run right into goon number three, whose weapon is pointed at the floor as he fiddles with the charging handle, trying to clear a jam of some kind. With my gun already up and at high ready, I simply drop my finger into the trigger well, and start working it as I close the gap, the last round making a contracted spiderweb of powder burns on his cheek as I jam the weapon into his face. His eyes are now open wide with surprise and fear. His body melts away from me and I continue to move and scan the room for more threats, first high and then back at baseboard level, making sure no one is crouched down out of normal line of sight.

It was completely stupid of me to charge a target. There's no need to close the gap when your bullet will get there twelve-hundred-feet-per-second!

I continue to flow through the little lobby area toward the T-hall in front of me. Backed safely into the right-hand corner, I own this space. With time and opportunity I perform a reload on the carbine, then the handgun, even though I had only fired four or five rounds. I re-holster the pistol and take another deep breath. Always important to keep them topped off given the time. Never good to *need* to reload in the middle of a firefight.

A shadow passes my peripheral vision, and my heart stops as my blood turns cold. Even the Beast turns to look at what floated through the doorway. My mouth hanging open, I hear in my mind a voice that never spoke before: "It is I, your old friend Death!"

I neither laugh in his face, nor cower in fear. He is here. *For me.* But first I have more work to do. I must save Keira—then he can have me. But not now, not yet. I stare into Death's eyes and find recognition. I am staring back at myself. Death falls in beside me with a nod, gripping tightly his wicked-bladed sickle, and the Beast moves in front. What a team we are—not quite a Fire Team of four, but still a team to reckon with.

There is a known threat in a room down the hall to the left, blocking my path to the third floor where Keira is being held. I need to check the right-hand T-hall. You can't openly put your back to a potential threat and expect to live. Time for dynamic movement and violence of action!

I pie the door frame facing right down the T-hall, leading with my weapon up and out, the skeletal stock up over my shoulder, reducing its length as I exit the room. Nothing in sight, so I swing around facing left toward the known threat. Nothing is visible but the wide-open marble stairway at the end of the hall, just past four rooms, with doors on either side of the wide hallway. The Beast and I race forward at top speed, Death a step behind me, moving hard for the stairs, breaking every CQB rule I was ever taught about passing threat doors without clearing the room. But, in an Active Shooter situation, you move as quickly as possible to the known danger at all cost, because your life is expendable. The hostage's isn't.

Especially when it's your daughter.

I do not plan to own this floor, let alone the building. It would take far too long for a single man to clear it properly. I have work to do, and surprise—dynamic movement and violence of action are all I have at my advantage.

As I race down the hall, past rooms, I come to the last room on the left, and out steps an oversized goon, his face smeared with sweat and blood. As I close the distance, I can smell his putrid sweat of fear. He is bringing his weapon to bear, but I am too close and moving too fast. We crash into each other and our carbines are pinned between us. My right hand gets trapped on the receiver against his oversized stomach, and my left is dropping down and back to retrieve my six-inch SOG serrated combat knife. His breath reeks of old coffee and hot peppers, and his eyes are bloodshot. My left hand comes up and back down in a single arc, slashing at his exposed neck. His eyes go wide as the Beast slashes and stabs frantically at his neck. The voice that never speaks fills my head with the thunderous sound of "Kill it ... before it kills you!" I can feel Death's grip on my shoulder, His cold hand digging into my vest.

The goon falls away screaming as more men rush the doorway. I race forward to the stairs. I hear shots and shouts behind me as men come out of the room, tripping over their downed companion. I never slow or break stride—my only salvation being to reach the stairs and make the corner!

A round strikes me heavy in the middle of my back. The ceramic plates take the round and protect my vital organs, but the shock wave from a thirty-caliber moving at 2,600 feet per second, at close distance, shakes my very insides.

I take them two at a time, the Beast leading the way, and my old friend Death floating along behind me. I round the landing and continue to the second floor. I hit the old marble hallway and slide to a stop fifteen feet down the hall, rolling over and lying flat out as close to the floor as I can get, my carbine lying flat with my eye pressed up into the Holosun red dot, watching the stairs.

The Beast stands, slightly hunched over, watching my six, while Death leans against the wall, watching and waiting. Knowing his time will come.

Out of my peripheral vision I see the steps to the third floor, but my eyes are focused on the stairs coming up to this floor. When you're hunting men, one tends to look for vertical shapes and forms. Being horizontal or lying on the ground at the top of a stairwell can provide an advantage—you will see their head before their weapon is high enough to engage you. Few men lead with weapon, eyes, head. Most don't wish to block their view of what is ahead with the weapon at high ready. This fraction of a second is all I'll need to hold this entire floor. That is, assuming all Wavy-Hair's men were on the first floor springing the death trap, and none are behind me. Certainly the Beast would provide warning if one came out of a vacant room.

I hear a pair of heavy boots taking the steps two at a time. Someone must have figured I was going all the way up instead of lying in wait for anyone who follows me. I see half a torso as a goon lunges up the pair of stairs sooner than I expect him. I trigger two fast rounds into his thoracic region, and he crumples from view and flops back down the stairs.

Death fills my brain with the sound of "Frag!," a twisted smile on his face. He must have seen it coming. The frag bounces off the wall and skitters across the marble floor just out of my reach. As I swing my lower body around to try and kick it away, Death flicks his sickle like a hockey stick and sends the frag back down the stairway. An enormous boom shakes me to my soul as broken pieces of plaster rain down. Whomever had tossed that frag was certainly not coming up those steps. I glance over at Death and my mind is filled with his voice: "Your death, their death, I care not ... just for death."

I am up and racing toward the third-floor stairwell. I pause at the first landing. I hear Keira shouting out a description of what is ahead for me: "Three men, large empty room." I hear an angry curse and she is muffled quiet.

I would rather not charge upstairs and into a large room with three heavily armed men in it, although really only two—one will certainly be next to Keira, controlling her. Two primary threats to get past, then a standoff of sorts.

On my vest I carry a small green smoke canister to indicate the "all clear" after an engagement, which can double as cover smoke. Also on my vest is a flash bang—not the cool police bangs with the three-second fuse, but a 12-gauge blank round that puts off 180 decibels of sound and bright flash upon impact. It's pure "throw and go bang"!

I pull the smoke canister and it ignites. Knowing it will take time to fully engage, I tuck it back into my pouch as I pull the pin from the flash bang.

Grabbing the now fully engaged green smoke with my right hand, I lob it up the stairwell and into the large room. My right hand drops to my carbine, bringing it single-handed up to my face, the red dot floating in front of my eyes. My left hand lets fly the flash bang, and I follow it up the steps, two at a time, hugging the far-right wall, expecting rounds to come through the smoke in the middle of the wide staircase. The bang and flash are impressive in an enclosed space. The aftermath and effects are just taking hold as I hit the last step.

My carbine is up, left hand as far forward as I can reach for stability, butt stock away from my body so my movement does not knock it out of High Ready. The red dot scans for targets while the Beast leads and, to my left, Death follows close behind, his cold breath on my neck. The little hairs there stand straight up as I know he is about to snatch my soul with a laugh and leave my lifeless body bleeding out on the tile.

As I reach the landing, the Beast roars a scream so frightening the man on the left of the stairway goes white. I can see the fear in his eyes. Can he see me as the Beast, coming toward him? This slight hesitation is all I need to pump rounds into his chest and face.

The green smoke is thick and doing a great job of limiting visibility in the large open area. Rounds are coming straight into the smoke toward the quiet thudding sound of the 9mm carbine running rounds into his teammate's face. I narrowly escape the barrage of rounds, and head toward the right-hand wall. If I overshoot my position, I may put Keira in my line of fire. I simply cannot engage until I have a clear view of her position.

I crabwalk forward, plates square on toward known threats, eyes floating over all I can see. I push through the last of the smoke to see Keira strapped to a chair, the dark-skinned man with waving hair standing behind her. My muzzle floats over the top of her head as my finger moves into the trigger well. Out of the smoke to my left comes the number two goon, crashing into me. His force knocks me off my feet. I slide on the marble floor, losing my grip on the carbine.

Rolling off my right hip and up onto my knee, I draw my handgun in a blur of motion, dumping round after round into the charging attacker. His vest sucks up the rounds as he closes the gap, bringing his carbine to bear. Adjusting my angle slightly, I drive two rounds into his T-Box, ending him in an instant. He crumbles lifelessly in front of me and Death is at his side, whispering in his ear, his eyes unblinking as his life force is taken from him.

Heavy pressure strikes my front plate, and a searing pain tears at my left shoulder. Rounds are coming in fast—and with accuracy. Rolling away to my right, back into the diminishing green smoke, and rolling over flat on my stomach, I return fire. Keira, knowing what to do, has bent as far over and out of the way as the ropes will let her, providing me plenty of target to hit on Wavy Hair. I send a double tap down range into his chest and my remaining rounds into his T-box.

Within seconds, my bloody SOG serrated knife is cutting away the 550 cord from Keira's wrists and legs. As soon as she is free, she leaps up and hugs me hard.

Still feeling the fear of the fight and not knowing who may be left alive, I push her away, snatching up her former captor's handgun. I hand it to Keira. She press checks the chamber, drops the mag for a round count, reseats the mag, and comes to SOL carry position, hands folded across her chest, firm right-hand grip on the weapon, barrel facing the ground, elbows tucked to the sides. With just a slight movement of the wrists the gun can be up and in action in a fraction of a second, yet it permits you to move around safely without flagging anyone with your muzzle.

"Are you with me, Keira?"

"I'm here, Dad!"

I rattle off a series of instructions, for me as much as for her. "Extreme prejudice is the only way out of here! We must kill them all! Shoot, move, communicate ... Reload once you're dry. Fall in behind me, grab my vest, and stay tight. I have more rounds than you. If I go down you must get to my gun and fight. They will not give you quarter! My spare mags are on my side and one on my vest."

Keira asks, "GeeZus, Dad ... You're sure?"

"Yes! But you must have the conviction to do so and to fight on no matter the outcome!"

"Okay, I will. I promise."

"Ready? Remember to slice the pie on every corner, check your near corner, sweep high, then sweep back low. Tap up."

She smacks my vest twice.

I respond, "Moving!"

"Move!"

As we step out of the main door we had separately entered not so long ago—which feels like a lifetime—we can hear sirens heading in our direction. We move over to the heavily shot up armored G-Wagon. Keira surveys the damage I have done, and what was done toward me. She looks at me, speechless. I ignore the look, stripping gear from my sweaty body. The pain is starting to set in. I remember the shoulder hit. Blood is running down my chest. The round was high and cut a lot of muscle, but there are no broken bones. The plates held up to a number of rounds. I drop the carrier into the back of the wagon. We dump our guns beside my kit and step away from them as the first patrol car, lights and sirens at full, turns into the parking lot.

Turning to Keira, I say, "Hold your hands away from your body. No need to make anyone nervous. They are going to handcuff us, separate us, and put us in different cruisers. If they ask you questions, just tell them you don't feel well and want to go to the hospital. You have something like three days before you have to give them your statement. But anything at all that you say can be used against you."

Two officers get out. I don't know either of them, which would have been nice. With running a law-enforcement training company, I meet a lot of cops, but there are still many more whom I have never met.

There's a fair amount of carnage. Two visible dead guys, two shot-to-shit vehicles, us two standing there, no visible weapons. These two could be cut from the same mold—both six feet tall, borderline bulging of muscles, one in a crew cut and the other almost shaved.

Baldy says, "What is going on here?"

Keira starts to speak. I cut her off. "Just wait until Philip Daniels from FinCEN gets here. He'll work this out with you guys."

Crew Cut says, "Come over here. We are going to pat you down and cuff you for your own safety." I tell Keira to go ahead and comply. Once cuffed and patted down, they lean us against the cruiser and start asking questions.

At this point, two more cruisers pull up, sirens and lights also full out. The guys roll out, ready to go. A callout of "Shots Fired" always brings them in fast and ready for action. The two new officers on the scene are shouting to Baldy and Crew Cut about what is going on, getting a sitrep—a Situation

Report—and so on. They decide they are going to go in and clear the building. They all look over at me. I shrug my shoulders, wincing in pain from my wound.

It's at this moment, as things start to come down, that I realize that the Beast and Death are no longer here. In fact, I did not see them at all once the shooting was over.

I am sure that Death is happy. His score card got filled. Running the scene in my head, I count a total of nine dead goons. What the actual fuck! How on earth did I accomplish that in less than ten minutes in a three-story building?

Years and years of teaching and training. CQB gives a man the edge.

Of course, the Beast and Death did help.

One ambulance shows up, then another. I tell Baldy and Crew Cut that my daughter and I need to go to the hospital for evaluation. "Keira has been through excessive trauma and I have a tight pain in my chest and oh yeah ... I got shot!"

Baldy replies, "You two need to give statements about what happened here."

The two officers who went inside appear on the third-floor balcony and shout down, "All clear, except for a bunch of dead guys." They look sharply at me.

I say, calm as can be, "You will get your answers. Just get us the medical attention we need!"

They are not having it. Crew Cut says, "You are not going anyplace until the brass gets here and clears this scene. Medics will attend to your needs." He and Baldy walk over to stand under the balcony to talk to the guys inside.

Medics come up and start working on us, even though we are cuffed. Keira is not physically hurt, but being abducted and nearly killed will have a lasting impact on us both. I am sure I will live, but, never having been shot before, it's a rather strange feeling of numbness and pain mixed with moments of panic. All the training in the world cannot prepare you for a real-world engagement.

Soon enough, the big man from FinCEN, Philip Daniels, shows up in his blacked-out Suburban. He stalks by me, walking around the scene, before going inside. A few minutes later he appears on the balcony, looking down at me, staring intently, before heading back inside.

As I zone out while the medics bandage my shoulder, Mr. Daniels exits, coming to stand nose-to-nose with me. "What in the holy fuck happened here?"

"They kidnapped Keira, and held her here. They lured me under the guise of a new client referred by an attorney I know, and ambushed me upon my approach. I was not waiting around while they shot up my vehicle and hurt my daughter for your federal guys to get here."

As if on cue, a second Suburban rolls up, and a team rolls out, all kitted up in matching dark green gear. They come stalking over to hear what Mr. Daniels has to say.

With a head nod, the team leader gets Daniels's attention. He cocks his head sideways and indicates for them to check the scene out. They move off first to stop and look over the armored G-Wagon—which took nearly sixty 30 caliber rounds—then to the Suburban that I worked over, and those two dead guys, then on to the doorway ... I relive my dash as they pie the corners and head in, the last guy holding up as the first pair check out the dude just inside the doorway with the jammed AK and the contact wound to the face. The last man on the team, having seen the body, looks back my way. I can read his mind. *How did that old fuck kill all these heavily armed guys by himself?* They will never know that I wasn't alone.

Mr. Daniels screams, "We wanted him ALIVE! Long, lonely prison terms are what my department goes for, not *bodies*!"

In a low, measured tone I say, "You fucking used me ... and my *family*! Now use that federal badge you are so proud of and get these cuffs off of us!"

"I think that we badly underestimated just who the hell you are," Daniels says, pacing around in a circle away from me. "We may have some more work for you. There are plenty of other cases I have open that need a guy who can speak the financial jargon and operate if needed."

I shout back, "Fuck that! You nearly got us both killed!"

Crew Cut, after taking my cuffs off, moves over to Keira, who is listening intently.

Daniels says, "Take some time. Get some rest. My open cases are not all this hot. You may come to like this type of work."

Honestly, he was right. Nothing like near death to make you feel completely alive!

But not for my family. Never again could they be at risk of harm. It's far too much for my psyche.

Perhaps, if I traveled, had a new name, a new identity when I worked this type of thing ... Shit, would Sofia even let me do this type of work?

Same first name, similar last name ... Hell, I could scour the medical records and do what the bad guys did—find someone about the same age and assume their identity.

But damn, these feds need to start paying me for my time and expertise. This bribery shit has got to stop!

CHAPTER 37
AN UNEXPECTED OFFER

A middle-aged woman escorts me down a hallway of windowed rooms in the Cleveland Federal Building, their frosted panes of glass obscuring who is in them. I'm led into a large conference room and, as I step past my escort, I read her name tag and security badge. I thank Donna by name and head for the coffee pot as a distraction and form of comfort. GeeZus, I'm tired. Always so tired. I add creamer and, as I turn, Philip Daniels comes through the door. He dismisses Donna from watching over me, and she pulls the door closed on her way out.

Philip lays a couple of large files on the table, comes around the table to get some coffee, and says, "I may never get used to not shaking people's hands again. I come from a background of close personal introductions and with this virus running rampant all over the globe and social distancing, I may never be the same."

Always the smartass, I say, "As long as we don't hug each other or lick door knobs we should be okay." Philips looks at me, cocking his head. I'm not sure if he thinks I'm a little daft in the head or funny.

"Before you tell me why I'm here," I say, as pleasantly as I can, "how about you update me on where things stand with Rajesh and his buddy Chance?"

Nodding, Daniels says, "Fair enough. We checked the phones we got from the dead guys. Of course, the phone company would not unlock them for us, so we had to wait for the court order and then for the company to get around to sending us the phone numbers of sent and received calls. Damned frustrating that we cannot get cooperation from the telecommunications industry on high-priority concerns. Just think of the text messages and photos in that phone we could benefit from. Once we got all the records, we did a quick search for Chance Richardson and Rajesh Nambootri Nimbalkar's numbers to see if either had made contact. We found that Chance had contacted one Jean-Pierre Buteau, a British National by way of Haiti through humanitarian efforts after the earthquake in 2010. Not much else on him ... some run-ins with British law but nothing linked to terrorist cells."

"How about Rajesh?" I tentatively ask.

"No. His number was only traced to Chance. I *can say* the dates and times link up close to Rajesh's calls with Chance and Chance's calls to Jean-Pierre, but that's the best we could do with the rules we are required to live by."

"So, are you thinking he's clear of all this kidnapping and trying to have me killed mess? Just some stupid kid selling pot to make a few bucks?"

Daniels shrugs. "Could be we will never truly know, but all the players certainly had contact with each other in some form or fashion. For you to consider this Rajesh as a non-threat would be a serious misjudgment on your end, but it's your life." After waiting a second to let his advice sink into my brain, or so I imagine, he continues. "We had local sheriff's office detectives try to pick up Chance at his place in town. No car in the drive, and no answer at the door. We then spent a few weeks getting a search warrant. We went back and served that with a staple gun to the front door. Nothing of interest in the house. Chance may have gotten spooked once Jean-Pierre was killed. Certainly no good reason to stay local."

"If Chance and Jean-Pierre were that close, I would have thought Chance would have been at the building where they took Keira. Maybe he's just a mule and not a hitter."

Why do I care if Rajesh and Jean-Pierre are connected? What difference does it make? I ask myself. *Well, for one it speaks to how well you read someone and second, your inner nature to want people to be good, even if it seems they may not be.*

I ask aloud, "Any clue where Chance ran off to?"

"BMV said he was a Michigan resident before he moved to Ohio. Could be he went back there to hide out and let things blow over."

There it is again. Michigan. The vehicle of the guy who jumped me so he could "teach me a lesson"—it had Michigan plates. I'm sure of it.

There was never any connection between Chance and me. It had to have been through Rajesh. Fuck ... maybe he *is* a bad human! His poor mother and uncle. I can't imagine.

"Any reason to pick up Rajesh?" I ask.

"Nope. We still have the currency transaction report and are still hoping to connect it with some drug dealing for a longer sentence. We have nothing to clearly connect him to this. If we bring him in it will just spook him and we may end up with nothing of any great value at all."

"This system is really fucked!"

"There are days it seems that way."

Before I can respond, there's a quick double rap on the frosted glass door and someone opens it without waiting for a response. A young guy in his mid-thirties steps halfway into the room and looks at Mr. Daniels. "Hey, Flip—don't forget that video meeting in ten minutes."

As his eyes settle on me, Philip nods in my direction. "Dan Smith, this is Trevor McCowen."

Dan steps all the way into the room, and says, "Oh ... hey. Nice to meet you, Mr. McCowen. I hear that you are a trigger God from the boys in green!"

Never sure how to take a compliment on killing people, I just nod my head. Suddenly the asshole comes out in me, and I say, "Flip—I mean, Mr. Daniels—do you guys all come up with fake names for work?" He looks at me with surprise.

Smith smiles and says, "Hey, see you both later," pulling the door closed behind him.

Shaking my head, I ask Flip, "You drag my ass all the way up here for a ten-minute meeting?"

"No. You will be in on that call along with everyone else." Pointing to the stack of file folders in front of him, he says, "These are the new targets. The entire team will be briefed on these threats, and that includes you."

Surprised, I ask, "In what capacity would I be on a federal FinCEN team?"

As I suck down my heavily creamed coffee, Flip says, "This is where it starts to get big and real—not only for you, but for us. The brass has not decided if you are going to become an employee/consultant or a subcontractor. Some of that depends on you and some on the level of liability we want to take on having you."

Sweet GeeZus! I wonder how this is going to read on my FINRA U-4 Disclosure Form. I can see the questions now:

i. Describe your Outside Business Activity: Hunting money laundering with the Treasury Department through FinCEN.
ii. How many hours per week will this activity require: As many as The Man requires
iii. How many hours during the work day will this activity take: See above
iv. What compensation will you receive for this service: Probably nothing but a pat on the back and a kick in the ass.

Flip opens the file on top and reads off a name ... my mind fades off toward our last "job," which we finished two months ago. My shoulder is nearly healed from the bullet that cut through the meat of my shoulder. My daughter Keira and I are both still seeing federal counselors provided by and paid for by FinCEN. We have both spent more time on the range honing our shooting skills, both knowing that the mind is a far more important a weapon than gunfighting skills, but the desire for actionable activity is so great that we must do something, and shooting seems to fill the void.

Damn, I'm tired. Always so very, very tired.

But, as we sit down to the video meeting and I meet the team, I think I could get used to this gig.

EPILOGUE

"SOUP"

My face is tilted back, eyes closed, facing the heavens. The sun is bright and warm today. Not yet hot, but that warmth that makes you feel somehow ... whole.

This second-generation-owned Italian restaurant has an outdoor seating area, a half wall around it, forming a courtyard effect that muffles the sound of traffic from the main drag. "Soup," a retired county sheriff's deputy and lifelong friend, eats here every day.

Even though it's still early—11:30 am—a beer sits in front of him. A coffee with cream is front and center on my placemat, as I enjoy the sun on my face. I shift in my chair to stop the grip of my handgun in its high-rise pancake holster from digging into my kidney.

"How is Keira doing?" Soup asks.

I reply with a nervous hand roll and shoulder shrug. "Not sure. She moved back home indefinitely. We've been to counseling a number of times. Seems good to me, but just not sure how deep-rooted that kidnapping and shootout got into her head from a psychological standpoint. I *can* say that she has been beating the fuck out of her body opponent bag punching dummy. BOB even has some very high-placed kicks to the chest imprinted on his torso."

Soup nods and takes a pull from his beer. Our waitress brings our lunches, setting them in front of us. A salad with grilled chicken for me and a cheeseburger and fries for Soup who thanks her by name. She smiles and says she will refill our drinks in a moment.

As she moves through the door, Soup asks, "You do know that regardless of the amount of therapy she gets, it will not change the reality of what she lived through?"

"I know. I'm just hoping to reframe it so that it doesn't haunt her for life."

"Do you think you made a difference?"

I jerk my head up sharply, giving Soup a hard stare. "Did *you* make a difference when you caught that planeload of pot back in the '70s?"

He says, "I actually thought so at first. It took a few years to understand how far and deep the greed really goes. I was very surprised by who all it touches."

"I'm glad I could play my part. But I'm not sure how you did it for thirty-plus years."

We grow quiet as the waitress sets another beer in front of Soup's almost empty bottle and refills my coffee, adding a pile of creamer cups to my saucer before leaving us to our meal.

ABOUT THE AUTHOR

Doug Emery has run a successful investment planning company for thirty-plus years. He and his wife Melissa live on their farm in northeast Ohio where Doug has spent a lifetime raising sheep, running bird dogs, hunting, and shooting skeet, long-range rifle, and doing Combative Tactical Firearms Training.

He works security through Belltower International, holding a Class A license in investigation and security.

Doug is the founder and president of North Coast Peace Officer Training Foundation (NCPOTF.org), a not-for-profit law enforcement training company, providing training at no cost to the officer or their agency.

A RosesTouchPhotography.com

For information about the North Coast Peace Officer Training Foundation and to buy merchandise to support the cause, visit https://www.ncpotf.org/

For information on Battle Tribe, visit @mattrendar on Instagram

Trevor McCowen's story continues in *Range is Hot*, coming soon.